THE TARNISHED BADGE

After three days on the trail of murdering bank robber Jake Worthy, tensions and infighting threaten to splinter the hastily-assembled posse from Quirt, Arizona. Sheriff Fawcett must turn back at Yavapai Creek, for his jurisdiction ends at the county line; should the men continue without him, they will lose their legal authority and become nothing more than a roving band of vigilantes. But the temptation of getting their hands on the stolen cash is enough to make them cross the water and run Worthy to ground . . .

Books by Logan Winters
in the Linford Western Library:

OVERLAND STAGE
INCIDENT AT COYOTE WELLS
DARK ANGEL RIDING
ROGUE LAW
THE LAND GRABBERS
THE LEGACY
SMUGGLER'S GULCH
THE TANGLEWOOD DESPERADOES
THE KILLING TIME
TRAVELIN' MONEY
MYSTERY HERD
THE RELUCTANT GUN HAND

LOGAN WINTERS

THE TARNISHED BADGE

Complete and Unabridged

LINFORD
Leicester

First published in Great Britain in 2013 by
Robert Hale Limited
London

First Linford Edition
published 2015
by arrangement with
Robert Hale Limited
London

A catalogue record for this book is available
from the British Library.

ISBN 978–1–4448–2503–9

Published by
F. A. Thorpe (Publishing)
Anstey, Leicestershire

Set by Words & Graphics Ltd.
Anstey, Leicestershire
Printed and bound in Great Britain by
T. J. International Ltd., Padstow, Cornwall

This book is printed on acid-free paper

1

The posse had gone bad. That was the best way Riley could find to state it on the third day they had spent on the blood-trail. Each of them shared the common conviction that Jake Worthy deserved to be dragged back to town in irons and hanged for the killing of Abel Skinner — a meek, harmless man who had never been known to carry a gun. That this had occurred during the robbery of the Quirt, Arizona bank lent some fire to their determination.

The six men had ridden out of Quirt on Thursday, followed the killer's tracks up the Whaley cut-off and down the far side of the mountain onto the Siskiyou Flats, a long, harsh stretch of country where white playa, baked hard by the constant sun, crackled under their horses' hoofs and reflected its heated light into the riders' eyes.

A day and a half on the desert brought them into the Thompson Gap area which was brush country, all dry and twisted chaparral, thorns and cactus with little grass and only occasional pools of brackish water for the wearying horses. Tempers had begun to grow short by the third day.

Lester Burnett was a granite-faced man who rode wearing a twill suit and black town hat. He was some sort of big shot in Quirt, the president of the Merchants' Association. He had been in an unpleasant mood since they had started after the bank robber. Now he was furious, spittle dribbling from the corner of his mouth as he muttered curses.

Sheriff Fawcett, riding at the posse's point, turned in his saddle and demanded to know, 'What in hell is going on back there?'

'Bean's pony is nipping at my horse. Do you know how much this horse cost me?'

Fawcett grunted unhappily. He must

have heard half a dozen times since Burnett had purchased the blooded white mare how much the animal had cost.

'Just separate them,' Fawcett said reasonably. There were any number of reasons a horse might nip at another. One, because they had been too close for too long. Also, sometimes one animal just took a dislike to another for no known reason, like men do. Or David Bean's stubby little dun pony might have been making romantic advances, horse-style.

'I'll stay well clear,' David Bean shouted with an edge of irritation in his voice. The homesteader was obviously offended by Burnett's complaint, possibly because it held an implied comment on the differences in their social standing. Bean, who was trying hard to scratch a living from the dry earth on his small parcel, had only joined the posse in hopes of receiving some sort of reward. He needed one badly. Just now, with his well only half-dug, he was even paying for water to keep his animals and crops alive. That was the reason he had been going to the bank at the moment the bank robber had burst from the front door and ridden wildly out of Quirt.

As Bean drew his pony away from the townsman's precious mare, Sheriff Fawcett's soup-strainer mustache twitched with annoyance. This was the reason he hated gathering a posse. It was all right if you had a planned objective with known fighting men, but these catch-as-catch-can posses, which had to be formed rapidly with whoever was at hand, were normally futile in his experience. What you got were a few angry men, a couple of kids seeking adventure, a few saloon-bum types with nothing better to do.

He should have let Leo Mather handle this on his own. Mather, the town marshal of Quirt, was a narrow, lazy-looking man who seemed always to have a sour taste in his mouth, judging from his habitual expression. Sheriff Fawcett had no idea what caused that expression, but he knew what was behind Mather's lazy appearance: the man was plain lazy.

'Well, Will,' Mather had told Fawcett in his office, 'you know this is a job for the county sheriff. By rights I can't pursue an outlaw past the city limits, and Jake Worthy is undoubtedly beyond those. You, on the other hand, are responsible for maintaining law and order across the entire county.' Mather shrugged as if he were pained by the situation. He wasn't. 'This falls into your lap, as sorry as I am about it.'

Sheriff Fawcett was more than sorry about it. He was sorry he had stopped off in Quirt on his way back to the county seat. The thing was, Marshal Mather was correct. It was Fawcett's job to find the bank robber, like it or not.

Mather would not even go so far as to release his only deputy to assist Sheriff Fawcett — just as well; Fawcett had seen the fat man who must have been somebody's brother-in-law. That left Fawcett to gather as many bodies as he could as rapidly as possible before the thief made it to Mexico or California, wherever Worthy was headed.

As a result, he now had riding with him the fussy Lester Burnett, who had probably never ridden a horse out of the sight of Quirt before, and the stringy David Bean, who was no horseman at all, but a plow jockey. Add to these Jesse Goodnight, who knew a few tricks of the trail all right. Fawcett had arrested the man about five years back for shooting a gambler over near Gap's End. Goodnight had done his time down in the Yuma prison and been released a few months ago. Apparently he had caused no trouble since then. But Sheriff Fawcett suspected that like many another 'reformed' outlaw, Goodnight had simply figured out how to be more careful in his work. Fawcett hadn't particularly wanted Jesse Goodnight along, but there hadn't been much choice; there were few volunteers to select from.

The other two had been signed up out of a saloon. Complete strangers to Fawcett. The tall man with the reddish-brown hair looked as if he had seen a little of hard times and rough weather. He had the cut of competence about him. The blond-haired kid with his nose already red from the sun might have just outgrown his playpen and been tossed out of his momma's house. Green was what he was. His name was Billy Dewitt, and he had attached himself to the tall man who had been in the saloon with him, though the two had been seated at separate tables. Riley, the tall man called himself, but it seemed to Fawcett that it was a name he had just picked up somewhere along the trail where his real handle had been jettisoned.

'There's going to be more complaints if we don't slow it down a little,' the man who called himself Riley said, as he rode beside Sheriff Fawcett.

'Yeah? And if we slow down, Worthy will get plumb away from us.'

Riley glanced at the riders trying to brush-pop their way through the mile of thicket. Blackthorn, nopal and mesquite grew in tangled profusion. None of the men had been wearing chaps, of course; Quirt was not in the sort of country that called for such gear. There would be a lot of cut-up trousers and gashed legs before this day was over. Burnett's prized white mare would have a few scars on its hide to show for the work.

'Mind if I ask you, Sheriff, why did Jake Worthy choose the local bank to rob when everybody there knows his face?'

'How would I know?' Fawcett growled unhappily as he tried to guide his gray horse up and over a rocky ridge screened by heavy brush. 'Maybe it was just the handiest. Maybe Worthy hasn't got any common sense. Maybe he knows that town well enough to know there aren't a dozen men with half a heart for chasing him.'

Riley only nodded. It was obvious to

him that Worthy had half a brain and that he did expect pursuit. Otherwise there was no reason for a sane man to ride into this wildwood tangle. No, the man was not stupid. Which left Riley's question unanswered. But then, who knew why men suddenly took it into their minds to commit crimes of any sort?

He let his concentration return to the rough ride upward. As they neared the crest of the gap, the brush began to thin to a more manageable obstacle to the riders, and they drew up at the ridge, looking down into a long, narrow valley, their horses standing in a shuddering line.

'I'll kill Worthy for that alone when we catch up with him,' Lester Burnett yelled. Glancing that way, Riley saw that the townsman's twill trousers were shredded and there were several long, bloody streaks across the mare's chest. Burnett was in no worse shape than anybody else, but he seemed to take everything personally.

9

True, the thorns had taken their toll on Riley's own horse and clothing, but like the rest of the riders except Burnett, he was wearing rough denim jeans and a red flannel shirt that were a lot tougher than Burnett's outfit. Besides, Riley reflected, his torn-out jeans could easily and cheaply be replaced — not so with Burnett's custom-made suit.

'That was a dirty trick, Worthy taking us through that tangle,' Billy Dewitt said. He was sitting his weary, scratched blue roan next to Riley. He had removed his hat to wipe the sweatband and the wind caught his wispy fair hair and made it look like a dandelion blowing on his head.

'It was,' Riley agreed, 'and I'll wager the man has a few more dirty tricks up his sleeve.' He smiled at the blond youngster. 'You weren't thinking that the bank robber wanted to be caught, were you?'

Billy grinned. 'No, sir, I wasn't. I guess these outlaws do have their ways.'

'They do indeed,' Riley said.

That brought Sheriff Fawcett's eyes their way. He fixed a glare on Riley and asked, 'You seem to be speaking from experience, Riley. Have you spent much time riding with posses ... or away from them?'

'We're wasting time sitting here,' the dark-eyed Jesse Goodnight said from the other side of the sheriff.

'We won't gain much ground on Worthy if we kill our horses,' David Bean said.

'The man's right,' Lester Burnett said, daubing at his white mare's scraped shoulder.

'Worthy's horse can't be any better off than ours,' Jesse Goodnight argued. 'We catch the man by keeping on, isn't that right, Sheriff?'

'I'm afraid it is,' Fawcett answered with a sigh. Turning to the others, he said, 'Look, men, I'm sorry as I can be about your animals, but we've ridden out here to do one thing — to run down Jake Worthy, and that's what we

11

are going to do.'

'It just doesn't make sense to me,' David Bean said.

Jesse Goodnight snarled a reply: 'How could it make sense to you, plowboy? You don't know nothin' but corn and hay and what to feed them with.'

The narrow Bean didn't respond. He looked bewildered, not understanding how he could have made enemies of both Goodnight and Lester Burnett in less than two days. Fawcett took charge again.

'All right!' the sheriff said, half-standing in his stirrups. 'This is how it's going to be. We're riding until it's too dark to see anymore. When we reach the flats, fan out and start looking for Worthy's tracks. We've got to track the man down before he reaches the Yavapai.'

Billy Dewitt looked questioningly at Riley as they started down the rocky flank of the hills toward the valley below. 'What's the Yavapai, and why is it so important to the sheriff?'

'Yavapai Creek is the recognized county line. The sheriff isn't supposed to cross to the other side hunting a man.'

Billy nodded, letting his eyes drift ahead to where Fawcett was riding a narrow trail down the rocky slope. 'Think he would? Pursue Worthy across the county line?'

'There's no telling,' Riley answered. 'It depends on how bad he wants the man, I guess. It's risking his job if he does.'

'Ah, no one could blame him for dogging the man's trail,' Billy said, 'county line or not.'

'Want to bet?' Riley replied as they finally reached the flat ground of the valley and lined out westward. At Billy's surprised expression, Riley went on, 'The sheriff's an elected official. All such have enemies that will try to use something against him if they want his badge. Suppose there is a big shoot-out, a murder or another bank robbery back in the east county? Men would be asking where the sheriff was when they needed him.'

'Well, no one would know,' Billy objected. 'None of us is going to say a word if he crosses the county line.'

'How do you know that?' Riley asked and Billy opened his mouth to respond, but fell silent. 'I don't know which side these men's bread is buttered on, do you? Besides,' Riley concluded, 'I see Sheriff Fawcett as a man who sticks to the letter of the law.'

'I suppose you're right,' Billy said reluctantly. He glanced toward Sheriff Fawcett, still riding at the head of the posse. 'No wonder he's in such a hurry to catch up with Jake Worthy.'

'That's it, and breaking down a few horses isn't going to cause him to slow down at all.'

'I guess not.' Now, as they noticed that they were lagging a little, they heeled their horses, lifting their pace to match the sheriff's.

The land they rode now was studded

with greasewood, some manzanita and clumps of nopal cactus. The valley floor was unusually flat, and Riley wondered if it might not have been under cultivation once. Perhaps the country had proven too dry, or maybe a man had tried to carve himself out too big a chunk of the wilderness, finding out later that he could not manage it all. As he was thinking that, he lifted his eyes toward a stand of six or seven live oak trees a mile or so away. Squinting, he could make out the angular forms of several structures hidden among and behind the trees, and now he could discern a patch of cultivated land farther along, perhaps forty acres which had been under the plow.

Urging his roan to quicker speed, Riley drew even with the grim-faced sheriff.

'Are we going to stop and talk to these people?'

Fawcett nodded. 'We'd better. I haven't seen a trace of Jake Worthy's horse since we hit the flats.' Riley shook his head. Neither had he seen any tracks of Worthy's mount. Fawcett told him, 'The land is open around here. They must have seen Worthy if he passed this way.'

'You'd think so,' Riley agreed as they approached the small collection of weathered buildings set among the oak trees, 'if they're the sort of people who notice things . . . and are willing to talk to the law about them.'

'We'll find out,' Fawcett replied, with a set expression on his face. He wanted Jake Worthy in the worst way, that was obvious. Either it was personal or Sheriff Fawcett just wanted to get the stolen money back to the people of Quirt, knowing how a loss like that could gut a small community.

The sheriff glanced at Riley, who continued to ride at his side. 'Was there something else you wanted, Riley?' he asked.

'I was just wondering if you had seen the man who's been following us.'

The valley they now rode rose to a

shoulder of broken foothills to the north and not once, but half a dozen times, Riley had noticed a lone rider following along on their westward route. Maybe there was an easier route in the hills, one that avoided the chaparral country and it was just coincidence that a local man was riding in the same direction as they were on that day. Yet there seemed little reason for the man to remain in the barren foothills when there was now easier travel and grass for his horse in the valley below.

Maybe the rider just wasn't the friendly sort; maybe the sight of so many silver stars glinting in the sunlight gave the stranger a motive to ride wide of them. Or, was it possible that it was their quarry, Jake Worthy, who now rode the hill country, having already lost his pursuit by veering off the trail in the thicket country . . . who rode now, laughing up his sleeve at the posse?

2

Scowling as he looked northward, Sheriff Fawcett finally replied, 'I don't see anybody, Riley. Your imagination is working overtime.'

'Maybe,' Riley was compelled to admit.

'Keep your eyes on the hills from time to time,' Fawcett said more affably. 'I guess all things are possible. If Jake Worthy is riding those rough hills, we could be ahead of him. Though it seems unlikely to me.

'For now, let's have our talk with whoever lives here — there's a lot of empty land around. They should have seen anybody passing.'

They dragged their way across the dusty yard in front of the small, weathered house. The wind off the west rattled the dry leaves of the oaks. At Fawcett's request Bean, Billy, Goodnight and Lester Burnett hung back, dismounting among the trees as Riley and the sheriff approached the house.

'Don't want to scare anyone,' Fawcett said to Riley. 'There's a lot of men out here who have had some trouble on their backtrails.'

Riley nodded his understanding. Before they had swung down in front of the gray house with the patchwork shingles, the front door had opened and a scrawny old man wearing blue jeans, red suspenders and a long-john shirt stepped onto the sagging porch, squinting in their direction. It was likely he received no more than a single visitor a year, but he did not seem happy to have company now.

' 'Mornin',' Sheriff Fawcett tried, touching his hat brim. The old man was looking toward the oak grove. He knew there were more visitors out there.

'What's the problem here, lawman?' the owner of the land asked. His voice was not friendly. Isolation makes some people suspicious of everyone. The old man had very bad teeth in front, both top and bottom. No wonder. Where was he to find a dentist out in this wild country? The nearest one Riley could think of was way down in Tucson. It was unlikely that this poor settler could even afford to have a tooth yanked. He must be living with constant pain. A toothache does nothing to brighten a man's disposition.

The man's wife had appeared on the porch behind him. She had a thick ring of fat around her waist, but her face appeared hungry and desperate. In an unconscious gesture she clawed at the air near her husband's arm.

'Nothing to get yourself upset about,' Fawcett said, trying for a smile. 'I'm the sheriff of this county, Will Fawcett, you might have heard the name.'

'Can't say I have,' the old man snapped. There were young kids around somewhere, for Riley heard the shrieks of some wild play near the back of the house.

Fawcett got down to business. Chatting the old farmer up wasn't going to work. 'We're looking for a man who robbed the bank over in Quirt. He must have ridden by your place. Tall man riding a buckskin horse — ' Fawcett was interrupted.

'Ain't seen him. Don't know if I'd tell you if I had. I don't like banks. Wouldn't keep my money in one.' The woman's clawing fingers finally reached her husband's thin arm and she gripped it tightly. Her wary eyes now seemed to hold fear. 'If that's your only reason for being here, I've answered your question and I'll thank you to leave.'

'Well?' Riley asked as they turned their horses back toward the oak grove.

'Well, nothing,' the sheriff answered. 'That was about what I expected. These old birds out here aren't known to be talkative. Too much chance of getting on the wrong side of somebody.'

'I wish we could have asked one of the kids — they always see what's going on and they're not shy about talking.'

Fawcett suddenly changed tacks. 'All right, Riley — where have I seen you before?'

'I don't know. If you remember, you tell me.'

'Your lips are about as tight as the farmer's, are they?'

'Sometimes. I don't like the idea of getting on someone's bad side either.'

'Does it work?' Fawcett wanted to know. 'Not talking to anybody?'

Riley laughed. 'Only sometimes.'

They rejoined the waiting posse in the dry shade of the oak grove. Fawcett looked around, mentally counting, and asked them, 'Where's Burnett?'

'He said he wanted to look at something,' Jesse Goodnight said with an elaborately bored shrug.

'And you didn't ask him where he was going?' Fawcett asked angrily.

'What do I care where the fat fool went?' Goodnight, who considered himself a tough man, shouted back at the sheriff.

'Either of you know where he went?' Fawcett asked David Bean, who was standing nearby, leaning against the rough trunk of a massive oak tree, and

Billy, who was squatting on his heels not far away.

'He didn't speak to me,' Bean answered.

'Didn't say a word,' Billy said.

'All right.' Fawcett removed his brown Stetson and ran a harried hand over his thinning dark hair. 'We'll give him two minutes to get back, then we're leaving. I hope the fool knows what he's looking for. That farmer won't take it kindly, and you can believe the old man has a shotgun just inside the door of his house.'

'Maybe he went to look for that buckskin horse Jake Worthy was riding,' Billy Dewitt suggested.

'The kid might have a point,' Goodnight said. 'Though I doubt that fool Burnett would think of anything like that.'

'You mean Worthy might have swapped horses?' Sheriff Fawcett asked, frowning slightly.

'Sure, if he could get one. He had enough money to convince the dirt-scratcher to do that, didn't he?'

'He did.' Fawcett asked Riley, 'What do you think?'

'Could be, but we've seen no horse tracks either in or out yet. A lot of these farmers don't like banks on general purposes. This one,' he inclined his head toward the farm house, 'wouldn't need any inducement to hinder us in our pursuit.'

'Me, I hate banks,' David Bean said. The farmer's face was intent. He slammed a fist against his saddle, startling the dun horse he rode. 'If Abel Skinner had come through with that loan for me, I could be back on my place right now instead of riding aimlessly out here.'

'He wouldn't let you have any money?' Fawcett asked, not unkindly.

'No. He said he'd give me the final word this morning, but told me that things didn't look good for me.'

'I guess you needed that money pretty bad,' Goodnight said. He was smiling in a dirty sort of way as he sat on his horse. It was almost like a predator watching its prey squirm, Riley thought.

'Hell, yes!' Bean exploded. 'It's live or die to me.'

'Is that the reason you're riding with the posse?' Goodnight prodded, refusing to let go of the entertainment.

'You're damn right it is. I'm desperate to make something out of this, maybe a bank reward or off a bounty on Jake Worthy.'

'Law officers can't receive either,' Jesse Goodnight said with a thin, wooden smile.

'I'm not a law officer!' Bean snarled.

'No? Take a look at that shiny piece of metal on your shirt,' Goodnight said.

'Well, then, what are you here for, Goodnight?' Bean demanded.

'Me?' the lean gunman said amiably. 'Why, I'm just a good citizen doing my duty.'

'Here comes Mr Burnett,' Billy told them. He pointed toward the farmhouse where Lester Burnett, leading his white mare, could be seen approaching.

'About time,' Fawcett grumbled. 'I wonder what he's been up to.'

'I couldn't guess,' Jesse Goodnight said, turning his head to spit, 'but don't the fat man look pleased with himself?'

'We'd better be ready to ride,' Riley believed. 'The longer we sit here, the more likely the farmer is to drive us off with his shotgun.'

That sent everyone into leather and they sat waiting for Burnett. The business owners' association president did indeed look satisfied with himself. It was difficult to tell why. Fawcett, on the other hand, was growing red-faced as Burnett dawdled. Riley was trying to mentally calculate how many miles Jake Worthy could have traveled while they wasted time here.

'Climb aboard that horse of yours, and let's get going,' Fawcett commanded sharply.

'I was just giving Dolly a little rest,' Burnett said defensively.

'Where in hell have you been?' Fawcett demanded.

'Did you see that big buckskin horse Worthy rode out of town?' Goodnight asked. Burnett, pulling himself into leather, looked befuddled by the question.

'Why? Is it here?' he asked in puzzlement.

'Never mind,' Jesse Goodnight snapped. He turned his horse's head and started along the valley road again. After a brief, pitying glance in Burnett's direction, Fawcett heeled his own horse forward. Riley and Billy, riding side by side, fell in behind, leaving a perplexed Lester Burnett and the angry David Bean to trail.

As they rode, the day grew hotter still and the road, skirting the cultivated fields, was bare. Dust flared up from beneath the horses' hoofs with each step.

Billy Dewitt had reversed his yellow bandana and pulled it up over his nose and mouth as Riley had done to combat the fine, filtering dust. Billy rode nearer yet to Riley and with diffidence now asked the older man, 'I notice that when the sheriff is trying to figure things out, he asks you what you think. Why is that, Riley?'

'No reason,' Riley shrugged. 'It's the same as talking to himself, I suppose.'

'No,' the blond kid said, disbelieving Riley's answer, 'I don't think that's it at all.'

Riley didn't answer the kid; he didn't even bother to shrug this time. A mile or so on, they reached open grassland which had never been turned with a plow, and the dust waned. Now, though it was hotter, the sun had canted over toward the low hills to the west, its light slanting harshly into their eyes. It would grow dark early and by sunrise, the land would be cold, rimed with frost. Riley let his eyes go to the northern hills from time to time, but there was no further sighting of the mounted man there. He asked Billy, 'Ever hear of any Indian camps around the area?'

'No, I can't say that I have, although I don't know the west county that well.'

'I never have heard of one either.' So

the rider was probably not a lone local Indian returning home, but someone who had trailed the posse from Quirt, which had been Riley's first impression.

The day dragged on. They no longer urged their ponies to speed, not even Sheriff Fawcett, who had the most to lose if they couldn't run down Jake Worthy soon. Rivers wondered if Fawcett had simply given up on catching the bank robber before they reached the Yavapai Creek, which marked the county borderline. Riding nearly beside Fawcett, but slightly ahead, Jesse Goodnight was bent over the withers of his horse, as if wishing himself farther ahead. Goodnight was not about to give up the chase, county line or not.

Was the one-time outlaw after the robber or the money Jake Worthy was carrying? Riley gave up trying to puzzle out these men and their motives. He had his own plan and his own duty to attend to.

The land had begun to rise again.

The slope was gentler, the brush more sparse, but the tiring horses moved upward with heavy legs. There was an hour's worth of sunlight left. Along the western horizon some color was already showing above the far mountains. Their pace had slowed, but it had nothing to do with flagging determination on Fawcett's part; they simply could not continue at a faster pace.

'I'm not having my horse die under me,' Lester Burnett called out. 'When are we going to stop?'

His voice was oddly muffled, and when Riley glanced that way he watched in disbelief as Burnett lifted a half-eaten sausage to his mouth.

'Where in hell did you get those?' Fawcett demanded, although he already knew the answer.

'Back at the farm. I came across their smoke-house.' Burnett's face looked suddenly fearful. 'Look, men! Don't get excited. I've got plenty to share. There's a long coil of them in here.' He patted his saddle-bags and offered them what he hoped was a placating smile. He still didn't understand.

'You stole from that farmer!' It wasn't a question the way Jesse Goodnight said it. He had slowed and turned his horse to face the townsman. Burnett's face was flushed with sudden anxiety. Goodnight's lean face was a savage mask.

Burnett tried again: 'Look, Goodnight, it's only a little food to get us along our way. Why would he miss it?'

'Probably because he works all year to store up enough food for the winter. So his kids will have enough to eat.'

'It's only some sausage,' Burnett whined. He was genuinely afraid now. Sheriff Fawcett, his own face dour, had drawn up beside Goodnight to let his horse shoulder the gunman's away.

The sheriff asked, 'Have you ever made sausages, Burnett? Do you know how hard that farm woman worked to make those for her family? No, of course you don't. You've never eaten anything that didn't come from a store.

You've taken food from that family's mouth, and they likely need all they can scrape together.'

'Sure, and that man will be mad as hell,' the farmer, Bean, agreed.

'So what!' Burnett, who now found himself surrounded by angry faces, shouted. 'I took some sausages. He sure isn't going to ride after us and start shooting because of that.'

Goodnight said in a cold, even voice, 'No, but as for me, I intend taking that road back to Quirt when I go. Which way are you going to ride, Burnett?'

'That man will have even less respect for the law than ever. I pity the next man wearing a badge who asks that farmer for help,' Fawcett said.

'There's nothing to be done about it now,' said Riley, who had been silent up to this point. 'We can't send him back. Let it go and let's keep riding.'

'That's all right to say,' Goodnight replied, 'but we will all have to ride back past that farm one day. If that sodbuster takes a notion, he can hide out along the trail and shoot us out of the saddle. For some sausages! I've a notion to shoot this dumb bastard down here and now.'

'You won't do that, Goodnight,' Sheriff Fawcett warned. 'I'd have to take you right back down to Yuma, and it would be for more than five years this time.'

'When the law won't do something, sometimes outlaws have to,' Goodnight said in a low voice, but his anger was ebbing now. He muttered something about it all being Jake Worthy's fault, and then swung his horse's head away, a bitter expression on his lips. They all knew that there was nothing to be done but to ride on and return their focus to capturing the bank robber.

'Where do you want to camp?' Riley asked Fawcett. 'The first place we see?'

'I suppose,' Fawcett said wearily. 'I was hoping we could find some water this side of the Yavapai, but it looks like there is none.' Side by side, the two men crested the knoll and started down into the valley beyond, which was cluttered with stacks of boulders and acre-sized stands of nopal cactus with some creosote plants and scrub juniper. The sun was no longer high enough to bother Riley's eyes. It settled slowly into its cradle beyond the distant high peaks. Neither was it bright enough to show the tracks that might have been left by a passing horse. Jake Worthy, to all intents, was lost to them in the night.

'What was that Goodnight was muttering about Jake Worthy back there?' Riley asked the sheriff.

'Goodnight thinks that Jake is the cause of all of his life's problems.'

Riley frowned, not understanding. 'Because he's led us out here?'

'Partly. You know that Jesse Goodnight just got out of Yuma prison after serving five years for manslaughter?'

'I'd caught the gist of it. I don't know any of the details.'

'Well, it was a dispute over cards. Goodnight followed the gambler he thought had cheated him, a man named

Adonis Klotz, out into an alley to continue the conversation. They got into it and Goodnight killed Klotz. Goodnight always claimed the gambler came at him, had a gun in his hand, and that Jake Worthy was there to witness it.

'Jake swore in court that he hadn't been there, hadn't seen a thing, and so Goodnight was convicted. Jake and Goodnight had been pals, you see, but they both had an interest in the same girl then. Believe her name was Bonnie Sue Garret. It doesn't matter. But Goodnight believes that Jake Worthy just wanted him out of the way so that he could have this Bonnie Sue to himself.

'It might be true,' Sheriff Fawcett added with a shrug. 'I wasn't there. But Goodnight still claims that it's true. Jake Worthy let his friend go to prison over a female. If Goodnight is the first one to come up on Jake Worthy, we won't have a capture, Riley, we'll have us a killing — one that nobody will be able to prosecute.'

3

They clustered around the low-burning campfire, trying to keep warm and keep their minds off their bellies, which — with the exception of Lester Burnett's — were cramped with hunger. The horses, picketed on the perimeter of the firelight, were in a foul mood over the lack of water. There was some graze for them here — dry, yellow grass — but they needed water to digest it properly.

The fire had been built using juniper branches. It was aromatic enough, but cast little warmth. The men's faces were in shadows cast by their hat brims. The fire flickered and wove in the light breeze which had come up with nightfall. Distant crickets could be heard chirping, though no one had been able to find a source of water which they would need. Maybe the melting morning hoarfrost provided enough for the crickets. Above, the night sky was cluttered with a trillion stars, sparkling silver against the black canopy of eternity.

'We're starting early?' Goodnight asked, but it was not really a question. If their intent was to outdistance Jake Worthy they had to spend more hours on the trail than the outlaw was willing to.

'Hour before dawn,' Fawcett said, letting the answer carry to each of the men. Weary men, saddle-sore men, hungry men. Each nodded, even Lester Burnett — who by unspoken common agreement sat well away from them in the shadows. No one had forgotten the sausages.

Jesse Goodnight finished the last of the coffee in his tin cup. They were thankful that Fawcett had been carrying a small sack of it in his rig. None of the rest of them had paused in their rush after Worthy to think of grabbing supplies. Stupid. But had there really been the time to spend? The thinking had been to get on Worthy's trail quick and ride hard. Like most mental images, this one did not pan out.

Goodnight had leaned back on one elbow, his tin cup still in hand. 'Jake Worthy probably had a steak and fried potatoes for dinner tonight. He had the time to make his plan. I believe he did get a fresh horse from that farmer. Now he's got a good lead on us and knows it, and he's planning on filling his belly at night and sleeping late in the morning.'

'You sound like you envy him,' David Bean said.

Goodnight fixed his dark eyes on the farmer. 'Do I? I envy him tonight, maybe. But I'll be alive tomorrow night and the night after that. I'd damn sure rather be me than Jake Worthy at this point. There's always time for me to eat and sleep when Jake Worthy can no longer do either.' The vitriol in Goodnight's voice was deep and seething.

Bean didn't answer the gunman. Instead he stretched out a leg and turned toward Riley. 'Mister Riley, do you know anything about banks?'

'Only a little, I'm afraid. Why do you ask?'

'Well, it's like this,' Bean said, 'I was trying to get a loan from Abel Skinner when the bank was robbed and he was killed. That leaves matters sort of up in the air as far as I'm concerned. If someone else takes charge of the bank, will my loan request have to be begun again, or will Skinner's recommendation — whatever it was — be acted upon?'

'That's sort of a complicated question,' Riley replied. 'It's a matter for the courts to decide if the bank will go into receivership and how the bank's obligations will be discharged. All of that has to take place at a territorial level. Those are things I don't know much about and probably wouldn't understand if they were explained to me.

'It will likely be a while before the bank is operating again,' Riley continued. 'Even if we recover what Jake Worthy stole, the Quirt Bank will be closed down until the auditors have gone over the books.'

Bean was not taking Riley's words well. 'But, why? If — '

'Because who knows, for example, that Worthy will be carrying all he stole? Maybe he has stashed some out, or split the money with an unknown accomplice. They'll have to find out if the bank's books balance before someone else can start operating it, if it has all the money it claimed to have in the first place. There are mistakes in bookkeeping as in anything else. And at times these mistakes are not accidental.'

'Abel Skinner was no thief, if that's what you're implying!' David Bean said loudly.

'I'm not implying a thing,' Riley said quietly. 'It's just that everyone concerned has to know what sort of footing the bank is on before someone new can take over. Think about it, Bean. Say you owe me forty dollars, and you tell me that you can't pay because someone stole twenty from you. How am I to know that? And then am I just supposed to forget about the money I'm owed?'

'I don't know,' Bean growled, pulling his hat over his eyes before stretching out on his blanket. 'I guess I don't understand it all — I just want my loan from the bank!'

'It'll be a while,' Riley had to tell him. These were the things bank robbers never thought about or cared enough to consider. Bean wasn't the only one in Quirt who would be hurting for a while with the bank closed.

★   ★   ★

Bank auditors. Those were the only words Lester Burnett caught out of Riley's explanation of matters to Bean. Those men from Tucson would come up and pore over the bank's books and discover many things, including the fact that Burnett had taken out three personal loans totaling fourteen hundred dollars. These were loans that his wife knew nothing about or his fellow members in the merchants' association. Only Abel Skinner, who had been the soul of discretion, knew of these.

The loans had been taken out only on the strength of Burnett's signature. He had had nothing to use as collateral except his character. A weak character it was. Lester Burnett had taken the first loan so that he could finance his next poker game, the one where he was sure to win back all that he had lost at that same friendly table. Losing again, he had approached Abel Skinner for a second time, and then a third.

It was at a private table that he lost, not in some public gaming hall, and so no one except Abel Skinner knew how far in debt he was and why. Burnett could not stay away from the cards! And if he did not go back to them he could never repay his debt. And so he lost again and again until desperation started to set in.

Only Skinner had known, but his financial woes might become public now; the new bank management might demand repayment. Just now, when Burnett had already made up his mind to run for mayor in the next election. Having his weakness made public could destroy any chance he had at the polls. And his chances had once been very good indeed with the entire merchants' association behind him.

Burnett had thought that capturing Jake Worthy and returning the stolen money to the bank would forestall any investigation of the bank's books. Now, if Riley was correct, territorial bank examiners would be swarming over the Quirt Bank whether Worthy was captured or not.

Burnett's political career was at an end. His finances were in ruins. He rolled over in his bed, furious and frightened at once. He lay on his back for a while as the fire burned low. He pondered — what did political office really mean to him except position and the ability to curry favor?

No, what really hurt him was the lack of finances. It was all about the money

— whether it was returned or if it could be somehow commandeered. He considered that closely, a thin ray of hope seeping into his troubled heart. Suppose they did not catch up with Worthy this side of the Yavapai and Sheriff Fawcett pulled out of the chase. What then? Who would be left if the posse decided to go on?

He might talk to Bean along the trail, suggesting a plan to him. Bean was as desperate as he was to make something out of this. The farmer was in need of money to keep his patch going. Who else? Jesse Goodnight had a criminal background. He seemed to wish to gun down Jake Worthy more than anything else, but surely a man like that would not object to splitting the bank loot with them. Then they could each go on their own way, perhaps start over in a new town.

The kid, Billy, he discounted. The blond young man was only in this for the adventure, Burnett thought. At any rate, the kid would not give them much trouble — not against three equally armed men.

Riley, he was a different matter. He fit no pattern that Burnett could discern. He seemed to be closer to Fawcett than was explicable. Maybe he would just give up the pursuit when Fawcett left and return to Quirt with the sheriff. That was something that could not be counted on, however. Riley was the one man that would have to be watched very carefully. But with Bean and especially the dangerous Goodnight on his side, Burnett thought there was no reason to worry about what Riley might do. If a plan could be designed before they reached the Yavapai, Burnett thought that there was every chance that he could wriggle his way out of trouble.

Lester Burnett yawned, half smiled and opened his eyes to the distant stars again.

The fire ring exploded as rifle shots struck the burning juniper branches there, spinning one of them skyward and showering Burnett with sparks.

David Bean let out a yowl and rolled from his blanket, which was smoldering. Goodnight cursed and automatically drew his pistol although there was nothing to shoot at in the darkness of the night. Billy Dewitt popped up from his bed, rifle in hand.

'Stay down,' Riley hissed at the blond kid as another rifle bullet struck the fire, sending a fresh shower of red-gold sparks skyward.

'Who's shooting?' David Bean called out.

'It's Jake Worthy, has to be,' Burnett called from the shadows.

'It's not Jake,' Goodnight said with conviction. 'No one's dead.'

'That damned farmer!' Bean said hoarsely. 'See what you've caused, Burnett!'

'Shut up,' Sheriff Fawcett ordered. 'Keep your eyes peeled for a muzzle flash, something to fire back at. He's near enough to pick us off one by one.'

'But who is it?' Bean asked again, his voice nearly a whine. 'Indians?'

Indians, Riley thought as he lay on his belly, clutching his Colt .44. Indians, or Jake Worthy. Or the wronged farmer.

Or the mysterious lone rider who had been tracking them for mile after mile across the lost land.

★   ★   ★

The fire burned low, the flickering tongues of flame withered and blew out in the wind. Curlicues of smoke rose in bleak surrender. The men lay unmoving for long, cold hours after the fire had burned out. There were no more shots; still no one was inclined to rise and move around. The sniper, whoever he was, might have been moving closer in the darkness all this time.

The sounds of Sheriff Will Fawcett outfitting his horse brought Riley awake in the dark chill of morning. No one had started a morning fire. They were all still jittery about the sniper. Jesse Goodnight could be made out, lugging his own saddle across the tiny camp.

47

Billy Dewitt was sitting up in bed, rubbing at his eyes. Bean moaned, 'Oh, God, not another day so early.'

Lester Burnett, who seemed to be in a better mood this morning, encouraged Bean with a few words, then rose stiffly from his blankets to equip his own horse.

'Time to mount up, Billy,' Riley said, passing the kid's bed.

'Yeah, I got the idea,' Billy said with a weak grin, 'I just don't like it much.'

Riley smiled faintly and walked to where his roan had been picketed overnight. Rime crackled underfoot. Riley rubbed his shoulders and shivered violently once. There was not even a hint of gray along the eastern skyline as of yet. There would be no breakfast, not even a cup of coffee, but they would hopefully be gaining ground on the elusive Jake Worthy. Smoothing the Indian blanket on his roan's back, Riley swung his battered saddle up. The small amount of movement got his blood circulating again, and as he slipped the roan its bit, he was starting to feel like a living man and not some creature that had clawed its way from its cold crypt.

'Be nice if we had some light to pick up Worthy's tracks by,' Riley muttered to Fawcett as he rode up beside the sheriff, who was blowing into his clenched hands to try to warm them.

'Hell, we haven't cut his sign for two days anyway,' Fawcett grumbled. 'We're just riding on probabilities.'

'Could be that he'll start to get careless now,' Riley said.

'There's that hope, but the man hasn't made a careless mistake yet. He's a cagey one, is Jake Worthy.'

With everyone mounted they headed westward once more. Not even the tall mountains ahead could be seen as yet. There was nothing but a dark land and dark men moving like specters along the ill-defined trail. Their horses' hoofs made splintering sounds against the hoarfrost, as if they were treading on glass. Riley heard Goodnight mutter, 'Jake Worthy's sitting up next to a fire somewhere, having a nice cup of hot coffee.'

No one replied; there was no response that could be made. Riley thought that Goodnight was probably right. How far ahead of them was the bank robber? He doubted that they had made up a yard of ground on Worthy since leaving Quirt. It was a defeated feeling, like running on a treadmill, that they rode with now.

One by one, forms began to make their appearance from out of the darkness. An isolated stack of boulders appeared and the tilted, solitary oak tree growing near it. Glancing across his shoulder, Riley now could see a gray band of light on the eastern horizon, and a flush of pink at its lower reaches. Dawn would come rapidly, but the air would remain chilly for some time.

Billy Dewitt's teeth chattered as he asked, 'H-how f-far to Yavapai Creek?' He had his shoulders hunched up to his ears in his thin leather jacket.

'I'm not sure, except that we should

reach it today. Then some men are going to have to make some difficult decisions.'

'At least my pony will have some water,' Billy said. 'What do you think, Riley? Are we going to cross the river and continue after Worthy?'

'I don't know. It's something every man is going to have to decide for himself.'

'M-me, I don't know,' Billy said. 'I've got nothing against Worthy. I'm not even from Quirt.'

'Do whatever you feel you must,' Riley said.

'You, Riley, what do you plan on doing?'

'Haven't decided yet,' Riley answered, although of course he had. He had to continue in pursuit of Jake Worthy. It was a part of his job.

That morning saw some strange companions on the westward ride. Lester Burnett was in close conversation with Jesse Goodnight although the gunman had only demonstrated contempt for the townsman. Before dawn, Riley had noticed Burnett riding near to David Bean, talking — although each had shown disdain for the other. Something was up, and Riley was pretty sure he knew what it was. The men were choosing up sides. The three had nothing in common except that one item which always attracted disparate men, temporarily bonding them.

Jake Worthy was carrying too much cash to be allowed to escape.

Sheriff Fawcett had undoubtedly noticed these goings-on as well. He was too experienced not to have seen them and placed the same construction on the muted conversations. Would that affect Fawcett's own decision about crossing the Yavapai into the neighboring county, illegally pursuing Worthy?

Riley decided things would fall out as they would. For himself, badge or not, he was going to track down Jake Worthy no matter how many miles, how much time it took.

As the sun rose higher and beat down on their backs they continued along the trail in torpid silence. Now and then Bean cursed at his slow-moving dun horse as it mis-stepped out of fatigue, but that was about it.

The sun was high overhead when they crested the grassy knoll and saw, unexpectedly, a little house of sawn lumber below, surrounded by a screen of cottonwood trees, their leaves flickering silver in the sunlight.

'Maybe someone with water and a kinder view of lawmen,' they heard Lester Burnett say.

'There's a chance,' Fawcett said, 'and it's worth asking. We won't see the Yavapai until nearly sundown if I'm not mistaken.'

Together then, they moved in a ragged line down the slope toward the tiny house. They had gotten to within fifty yards of it before a woman burst out onto the porch, screaming and waving her arms at them.

4

Riley, as amazed as any of them, slowed his horse and stared at the porch of the small house, where a woman in red silk continued to wave her hands frantically in their direction, dancing a sort of crazed jig as she tried to attract their attention.

She already had it.

She was young, dark-haired and slender. Now her voice reached them and they could make out a few of the words. *'Help!* Help me, I beg you. Please!'

Fawcett glanced at Riley and kneed his horse forward. The two men reached the porch as the hysterical woman stopped her frantic dancing and clung to an upright post, her slender arm slung around it. She looked up with grateful, dark-blue eyes, attempted a smile, failed and said in a dry whisper: 'Thank God.'

'What's happening here?' Fawcett

asked, taking charge.

'He . . . a man came to my house. Last night. He said he wanted food and a horse, and I could give them to him or he'd take them by force.' The girl hesitated. 'Of course I gave him what he wanted.'

'Did he give his name?' Fawcett wanted to know.

The girl shook her head vehemently. 'No, no name. He just displayed his pistol and told me what to do.'

'We know who it was,' said Jesse Goodnight, who had arrived in time to hear the last of the girl's broken words.

Fawcett scowled. 'What did this man look like?' he asked.

'Look like . . . ?' The girl sounded dazed. She took a deep breath, stood away from the porch support, smoothed her red skirt and thought for a moment. 'He rode a buckskin horse with a splash of white on its chest. He was fairly tall. He had a full, dark mustache and black eyes. And he was left-handed,' she told them.

'Jake Worthy,' Fawcett said, glancing at Riley.

'I knew it,' Goodnight said. He was appraising the young woman from horseback. It was difficult to tell his motives, though she was a good-looking thing. 'Which way did he go?' the gunman demanded.

The girl looked startled by the question. She stuttered an answer. 'I don't know . . . well, I do, but he told me . . . ' her voice became more panicked, ' that there were some men following him and if I said a word, he would know and he would come back and take care of me. I was so frightened. That's why I was so happy to see you men arrive.'

'What's your name?' Riley asked gently.

'Rita. Rita Poole,' he was told. With more excitement she said, 'I have to clear out of here, you can see that. What if he does come back . . . ? I have an aunt in Ellis. If I can get there, I'll be safe.'

'You mean you live here all alone?'

Fawcett wanted to know.

'Last winter,' she said, 'my father and mother both took ill with the diphtheria. I tried to nurse them through it, but in a couple of weeks they both died. I've been here alone since.'

'Tough,' Fawcett muttered, not without pity.

'I've got another horse, an old mare. As soon as I saddle her and grab a few things, I'll be ready to go,' Rita Poole said almost feverishly.

She had turned toward the door when Fawcett barked: 'Just wait a minute, Miss Poole. No one said we were taking you along with us. I don't even know if we'll be riding as far as Ellis.'

'That's where the man said he was going,' Rita said, whirling to face them. 'Don't you want to catch him? If I stay here, I'll be alone, at risk. Riding alone I'll be just a target. I was so happy to see six grown men with badges on their chests riding up. I knew I'd be safe then. After so much fear . . . Don't tell me that you aren't chivalrous enough to assist a poor orphan girl.'

'It's just that — '

'Of course we are,' Goodnight said. 'I, at least, will see you as far as Ellis.'

'That's across the Yavapai, isn't it?' Billy Dewitt asked in a quiet voice, and Riley nodded. That explained at least some of Fawcett's reluctance to promise the girl safe passage.

'Let me give you a hand,' Goodnight said, dismounting. He swung down from his horse and said to Bean, 'Maybe you can find the girl's mare and get it trail-ready. You all can water your horses at that tank.'

'Taking over already, is he?' Fawcett said through tight lips. 'It's enough to make me cross the Yavapai myself.'

'They'd have your badge for it if anyone found out,' Riley said.

'Who's going to say anything, Sheriff?' Billy asked. 'Not us, certainly.'

'No. Not you, at least, Bill, but Goodnight and Burnett might not be so close-mouthed. Burnett, especially, is entwined in county politics. If he thought it would gain him favor in some quarters to take me down, it's not beyond him.'

'I don't see why any man would do that to you just because you tried to do your job!' Billy said, shocked.

'Then you don't understand politics,' the sheriff said in a muffled voice. 'Riley, if they decided to cross the Yavapai, will you take charge for me?'

'You know I can't do that, Sheriff.

'I didn't think so.' The sheriff removed his hat and wiped back his lank dark hair. He looked suddenly older and slightly bewildered.

'I'll see if I can help inside,' Riley said, swinging down from his roan.

Now it was Billy who seemed puzzled. Why would the girl need the help of two men to pack up a few of her things?

'He just wants to look around the house,' Fawcett told Billy. That did nothing to clear the mists of confusion.

'Sheriff Fawcett,' Billy asked, 'is Riley — ?'

The sheriff cut him off. 'Whatever he

is, he'll tell you if he thinks you need to know. Let's just say he's a capable man. It took me a time to recollect where I knew him from, but now I remember. Stick by his side and listen to what he has to say and you'll be all right, kid. We'd better water our horses as well.'

Riley slipped silently into the house. He could hear the voices of Rita Poole and Goodnight in a back bedroom. They didn't sound like strangers. Frowning, Riley went into the kitchen, noticing that there were still dishes at the table from a breakfast for two. That didn't have to mean anything, but it was curious. There was much growing curious about this crossing of paths. He returned to the living room just as Rita Poole and Goodnight — carrying a leather satchel — emerged from the bedroom. Goodnight was glowering, but Rita had a bright smile on her face. The expression faded as she saw Riley.

'Did you want something, Riley?' the badman demanded.

'Just came to see when you were

60

coming,' Riley answered. 'The sheriff's ready to ride.'

'So are we,' Rita Poole said. She paused and looked around the house theatrically. 'It's hard to leave, no matter the circumstances.'

She turned back to look at Riley, her hands clasped, her eyes lifeless. All of the hysteria, the nervousness, the fear, was gone from her voice, however.

'Has Bean brought that mare around?' Goodnight wanted to know.

'Let's find out,' Riley suggested. The daylight was nearly stunning as they exited the dark interior of the cabin. The cottonwood trees surrounding the house flickered and waved in the breeze. David Bean had returned with an old animal which made even his heavy-footed farm horse look flashy. Goodnight eyed the mare with disapproval. Rita, wearing a light black jacket now, apologized to all of them.

'The man took Bullet, my three-year-old sorrel. The old girl here has been put out to pasture for years. She's all I have left to ride.' Rita Poole managed to produce a few tears which filmed her pretty eyes. She dabbed them away with a small, lacy white handkerchief.

'I only hope it'll stay on its feet long enough to get you to Ellis,' Goodnight said.

Everyone had noticed that Goodnight was speaking with more authority now. Lester Burnett asked timidly: 'Is that where we're headed? We're going across the Yavapai?'

'That's the plan,' Goodnight said, and Riley — who had been watching Burnett — thought he saw a small look of triumph or satisfaction cross the townsman's face. What was that about? Riley could guess, but he tried not to indulge in such sports. It was too easy to be wrong.

*　*　*

Silently then they wove their way through the cottonwood trees and traveled farther along the flat valley floor. Once, through a cut in a low-lying bluff, Riley saw a glittering flicker of silver like sunlight reflecting on water. They would reach the Yavapai that day.

The brooding Fawcett, who must have felt he had failed in some way, would have to make a decision soon, as would all of them. For once they crossed that river, in pursuit of a bank robber or not, they became simply a band of vigilantes without legal justification for any course of action they might choose.

It was a dangerous situation.

Glancing ahead, Riley saw Rita riding closer to Goodnight than he might have expected. The two were chatting, not without animation. Bean and Lester Burnett rode widely separate, yet they seemed to share a common optimism. Fawcett looked as if he were riding his last mile. Billy and Riley trailed, neither of them with much confidence displayed.

'Sheriff Fawcett said you might tell me . . . if you felt like it,' Billy coaxed

Riley as he rode nearer.

'Tell you what?' Riley said, looking away from the blond kid.

'That's what I don't know,' Billy persisted. 'What you are, who you are, what you're going to do at the Yavapai. You see, Riley, I have to decide too. Maybe it's best for me if I just ride back to Quirt with Fawcett. If I'm not a deputy any more, what do I care about Jake Worthy and all of this?'

'It might be the best idea,' Riley said.

'Does that mean you're not going to tell me?' Billy asked. 'The sheriff said that I'd be all right if I stuck by your side and listened to you. Well, here I am, riding at your side, but you sure aren't telling me much.' There was obvious frustration in Billy Dewitt's voice.

Riley considered for a few minutes, then shrugged. What difference did it make if Dewitt knew who Riley was and what had brought him here?

'It all started,' Riley said, 'just before my first bank robbery . . . ' Billy Dewitt gawked at him. Riley shook his head. 'Listen to me first. I was in a little town down south, Cannel by name.

'The day was summer-hot and I was beat down. Hungry — I hadn't eaten in two days. I was so dirty the town dogs would sniff and then detour far around me. I had no place to go and no money to get there with.

'I was standing in an alley just to get some shade from the buildings around me. My eyes settled on a little flat-roofed green building across the street. It had a sign on it, 'Merchants Bank of Cannel'. I looked long and hard at that little crackerbox of a bank, considering the possibilities.'

'So you robbed it?' Billy asked. He was almost breathless. Ahead now they could both see the narrow, silver-blue band of Yavapai Creek wending its way through the trees and willow brush. Riley didn't have much time to spin the yarn out. He told it as simply and quickly as he could.

'As I was standing there, a man

slipped up beside me. He was round, short, smoked a stubby pipe, and moved on his feet like a cat. I hadn't even heard him approaching.

''Hot and dry again,' is what he said to me. 'Have you got a match?'

'I wasn't in the mood for small talk, but he persisted. 'My name's Royle,' he said, lighting his pipe with the match I'd given him. I just told him I was pleased to meet him. 'Looking for work in town, are you?' Royle asked. 'Not at the moment,' I said, growing a little irritated with the man.

''I, myself am employed here,' the little man said. 'I work all around.' Royle waved his pipe, indicating a wide territory.

''What are you?' I asked. 'Some sort of drummer?' He shook his head, those shrewd little eyes of his squinted a little. He told me, 'No, my young friend, I am employed as an operative in the enforcement arm of the Territorial Bank Examiner's office.'

''Oh,' was all I could think of to say,'

Riley told Billy. 'Royle went on to tell me that his job was to track down bank embezzlers, robbers, wrongdoers of any sort associated with the banking business. He went on to explain that thieves thought they had lost the law once they had gotten past the town limits, left the county, crossed a state line.

' "The local law doesn't have the resources or the time to spend tracking them all down,' Royle told me. 'Me, I've got all the time in the world, son, all the time in the world.' Then he just turned and ambled off.

'I don't know how Royle could have known what I had in mind on that hot, dreary day, but if what he had said wasn't a warning, it was the next thing to it. I gave up the idea of robbing the Cannel bank.'

'And you never saw the little man again?' Billy Dewitt asked.

'Oh, I saw him again. That very night I walked to his hotel room and asked him if there was any chance of getting hired on to a job like his. I worked for him for years, until he retired. I still work for the Bank Examiner's office.' Riley paused and glanced at the riders ahead of them, at the near river. 'And I'm still doing the same work that Royle hired me on for.'

'You're after Jake Worthy.'

'More precisely I'm after the money he took. I don't even have the authority to arrest the man once we do find him. My obligation begins and ends with retrieving the money,' Riley said.

'But the thieves, the bank robbers,' Billy said. 'They can't often be willing to turn the money over to you.'

'Seldom,' Riley answered, 'and that's when the job gets interesting.'

They were starting down a grassy incline toward Yavapai Creek now. 'How did you even know to come up to Quirt?' Billy asked.

'I didn't. I was on my way back from up north and needed some rest. I stopped at Quirt and the stick-up happened. I figured I'd better join the posse. Otherwise I probably would have to have ridden back to Tucson just to be sent out again. To Quirt.'

'You live an exciting life,' Billy said with a trace of envy.

'Do I? It does have its moments,' Riley agreed. 'But it's damned tiring, brutal in fact. I travel far and hard and often it's for nothing.'

'Men do get away from you, then.'

'Oh, yes,' Riley was forced to admit. 'I've had them outdistance me, out-smart me and ambush me. Sometimes it seems that I've spent as much time on my back recovering from gunshot wounds as I have riding the last few years.'

'You're not married,' Billy said. It was a half-question.

'Yes, I am. We have a place down in Crater, a very small town without much to put it on anyone's map. My wife, Dusty, knows me well enough that she realizes if I ever had to stay at home and just sit on the front porch rocker, within a year I'd put a bullet through my own head, or she would have to because I'd be stark raving mad.

'Dusty has a lot of friends and a lot of patience. We've carved out an unlikely way to live, but it suits us.'

Billy nodded. Ahead he could see that Goodnight had already led his horse to water, as had Rita Poole. The two seemed to be in close conversation. 'That seems odd,' Billy commented. 'They're getting along famously for two people who have only known each other for a few hours. What do you think, Riley?'

'Oh, I think you have a point, Billy, and I believe I know what the secret to it is.'

'Can you let me in on it?' Billy Dewitt asked eagerly. Riley only shook his head. Others were within earshot now. Besides, the kid was probably better off living in ignorance. Seeing he was not going to get an answer to his question, Billy only asked urgently, 'You're crossing the river with them, aren't you? You have to, don't you?'

'I have to,' the tall man agreed.

'I'm going too,' Billy said with conviction. 'Would you do me one favor before we go on? Will you tell me what your real name is, Riley? I won't tell anyone. I won't speak it.'

'Laredo,' the man called Riley said. 'They call me Laredo.'

★   ★   ★

The western sky was a swirl of tangled color as low, filmy clouds were blown south across the sundown sky. Yavapai Creek ran deep and dark, its surface colored with reflected purples and deep reds. Sheriff Fawcett had already gathered the members of his posse on the riverbank, beneath the wide-spreading sycamore trees that grew there. As Billy and Laredo approached he whistled for the attention of the others.

'All right,' Fawcett began. He had removed his hat and now stood turning it in his thick hands. 'As you all know this is the point of decision for me, and no matter what my instincts prompt me to do, I cannot justify crossing the county line to follow Jake Worthy.

'You men are free to do what your consciences dictate, of course. I suppose you may as well hand back your badges since they mean nothing at all once you cross the creek. I release you from your honest effort on behalf of the town of Quirt and the county,' he said as if reciting some sort of set piece he had spoken often in the past. Probably he had.

There was nothing more to be said. Holding out his hat, Sheriff Fawcett gathered the badges that the men were unpinning from shirt fronts and vests. As they clicked together in his Stetson, Fawcett caught Laredo's eye and motioned with his head. Laredo nodded.

'Well?' Fawcett said as the last badge was discarded. 'Does anyone wish to ride back with me to Quirt?'

'I guess I'll go on with the others,' David Bean said, looking toward Goodnight, who had assumed the mantle of leadership now. The others agreed. Rita Poole stood watching them, the late shadows masking her expression.

'Billy?' the sheriff asked as if he were eager for a trail partner.

'No, sir,' Billy Dewitt answered. 'I believe I'll go along and see if we can't run Worthy down.'

'All right,' Fawcett said, removing the badges with one hand and planting his hat firmly with the other. 'Just remember, men, you're nobody special now in the eyes of any local law you might encounter. Your rights are only those of any private citizen. Bring Worthy in if you can. I know the citizens of Quirt would be grateful.'

'Grateful enough to offer us a reward?' Lester Burnett asked with a sneer.

'You'd know about that better than I would, Mr Burnett,' the sheriff said. He paused and said in parting, 'Boys, try to catch the man, try not to break any laws, and try to keep yourselves safe.'

They were pointless words. They had

already quit listening and were now gathering around Jesse Goodnight to await new instructions. Fawcett shuffled toward his horse, Laredo trailing after him as the sheriff had requested with his nod. Tightening his cinch, the sheriff spoke to Laredo across his gray horse's back.

'Think you can manage them, Riley?'

'No. No, I don't. I doubt that Goodnight even wants me along. It's his show now.'

'Yes,' Fawcett sighed. 'I can see that. I should have known this was coming — I guess I did.'

'I don't know what else you could have done,' Laredo said as the sheriff swung into leather. From the creek they heard a woman's laugh — short, merry.

Laredo asked Fawcett, 'Do you think that she is — ?'

'Yes, I do. Don't you, Riley?'

'I do, yes,' he nodded. He shook the sheriff's hand. 'Watch yourself going back along the trail — that farmer will still be good and mad.'

'I know,' Fawcett said, as his gray tossed its head, eager to be going. 'Him and that sniper.'

'He won't be bothering you any,' Laredo believed.

Fawcett's eyes narrowed. 'No? You've got him figured out now, too, do you?'

'I think so. If I'm right, he won't be looking for you, but he will be coming with us, and he's not going to quit until he's spilled some blood.'

5

Laredo walked back through the trees to the riverbank, expecting to find the men settling in for the night after the long dry ride, but they were too eager for that. Like hounds straining to be released from their leashes, their faces were flushed, eyes eager in the dim light of dusk.

'The girl's right,' Jesse Goodnight was telling the others from horseback as Laredo approached the group of men. 'Ellis is where Jake Worthy has gone. It's the only place along this trail. It's the only place he could be. He knows he's across the county line now, and he's got plenty of money to make himself comfortable with. We're going to drop Rita at her aunt's and then spread out and search Ellis. Look in the stables for those horses, look in every saloon and ask at the hotels. Because he's there — but if I have my way he won't be having such a comfortable time of it come morning. Mount up, boys, we're going snake hunting.'

Goodnight received what Laredo could only term a silent cheer for his speech. Eager, animated, the broken posse started across the Yavapai, set to make their fortunes from another man's blood.

Crossing the narrow, dark river they achieved dry ground again and were soon riding across country that was dotted with many live-oak trees, much scrub oak and sage. It wasn't a garden spot, but it made it seem as if the world had come to life again after some of the bleak land they had passed. The dusk provided only a narrow purple band along the mountain ridge when they approached the small town of Ellis. They rode more quickly now than they had for days, each man leaning forward in the saddle, eager and greedy looks on their faces. The gleaming lights from Ellis might have been so many glittering gold pieces, the way they were clutched at by their hungry eyes.

Goodnight drew them up at the outskirts of town. He announced, 'Men, first I've got to take Miss Poole home. To her aunt's house. The rest of you are free to treat yourselves to food and drinks.'

'I believe I'll ride along with you,' Laredo said and Goodnight's head spun toward him.

'We don't need you, Riley!' Goodnight said, with what was nearly a reptilian hiss.

'You never can tell,' Laredo answered evenly. 'We've brought the lady all this way safely, but there's still a dangerous man around somewhere. I'd feel better if she had more than one man escorting her.'

Jesse Goodnight's face had frozen its expression, but there was no argument to be made against Laredo's reasoning. Quietly Billy said, 'I'll go too.' He knew that some game was being played between the two older men. Although he didn't understand it, he didn't wish to miss out on its conclusion.

'Three's plenty,' Lester Burnett said. 'Me, I'm for whiskey and a steak.'

'That suits me,' Bean agreed instantly.

'All right, then,' Goodnight said, 'that's the way it is. Burnett, Bean — keep your eyes open, because Riley is right about one thing. Jake Worthy is still around.'

Then, without further words, Goodnight yanked his pony's head toward an intersecting lane and started down it, Rita Poole trying to keep up on her aged, tiring mare. Rita's face, in the brief glimpse Laredo had of it, was furious. Laredo and Billy fell in behind, riding silently. Billy had questions, but he held them in as they followed the dusty byway down into a narrow gully where sagebrush grew as high as a horse's head. They could smell water in the cool depth of the cut, but saw none. A mile or so on, the gully exhausted itself and flat land opened up ahead of them. They could see lantern light from the widely scattered cottages across the valley, beckoning home-comers.

Goodnight and Rita Poole did not speak now as they rode directly toward the second house they passed and into a yard where dry yellow grass grew, a single white oak flourished and a small black dog emerged from somewhere, furiously barking its warning.

'Shut up, Paco!' Rita shouted at the dog, but it did nothing to quiet it.

Laredo noticed a small wooden sign with a name burned into it hanging above the front door as it was swung open by a hunched, frail-looking woman holding a lantern.

'Who is it?' the woman's cracked voice called nervously.

'It's only me, Auntie!' Rita called out. 'Can't you do something to shut this dog up?'

Without speaking, Goodnight swung down from the saddle and untied the small satchels Rita had brought with her from her home. Taking them to the porch, he touched his hat to the old woman and turned away without speaking. Rita called after him, 'Goodbye, Mr Goodnight. Thank you, men.'

Laredo answered, 'Goodnight, Bonnie Sue,' and heard a snarl escape from Goodnight's lips before he spun his horse around harshly and rode away toward Ellis at a rapid canter. Grinning, Laredo led the way from the yard, leaving Billy even more perplexed. The little dog's frenetic barking followed them for half a mile.

'What did you call her?' Bill asked finally, no longer able to keep his curiosity in check. 'Rita Poole, I mean.'

'I called her Bonnie Sue. That's her real name. Someone had burned the name 'Garret' into a sign above the cottage door. I already suspected it, but the sign was enough proof to me to confirm that Rita Poole is actually Bonnie Sue Garret.'

'She sure gave you a funny look when you spoke that name,' Billy said, as they walked their horses up the dark road along the gully.

'I don't imagine she liked it very

much,' Laredo replied.

Billy could not manage his curiosity for long. 'All right, Lare — Mr Riley. Who is Bonnie Sue Garret and what makes her important? Assuming she is.'

'Oh, she is,' Laredo answered. 'But I don't want to lay it all out for you just yet. Can you wait awhile?'

'I don't know if — '

'If I buy you a steak and a cool glass of beer?'

'All right,' Billy laughed. 'You do know how to bribe a man. It's a good thing one of us has a paying job. I was trying to figure out how to come by a meal of any kind.'

'I'm buying. And I'll hire you a hotel bed for the night,' Laredo promised. 'You'll need a good night's sleep. I think tomorrow is going to be a busy day.'

'What's the first thing we're going to do in the morning?' Billy asked, as they achieved the flats again and Ellis appeared before them once more.

'The first thing we're going to do is

the last thing Jesse Goodnight would think of doing. We're going to pay a visit to the local law.'

'But why?'

'Because we're strangers in a strange town, looking for a bank robber and his take. There will be trouble before this is ended. It would be nice to fill the law in and let them know what side of things we are on.'

'I wouldn't have thought of that,' Billy admitted. 'I suppose you've had a lot more experience dealing with local lawmen.'

'Enough, and not always good experiences.'

'Meaning?'

'Some of them just don't want meddlers, troublemakers of any kind in their towns. Others' ears only perk up when gold is mentioned — and that can start a whole 'nother series of problems.'

'Maybe we should have held on to our deputy sheriffs' badges,' Billy said, thinking out loud. 'That might have given us at least some credibility.'

'No more than if Jesse Goodnight chose to wear his,' Laredo pointed out. 'No, Billy, we'll just have to see the town marshal, constable — whatever they have here — and be honest with him. Let him make up his own mind about us, while we consider what sort of lawman we are dealing with.'

Morning was bright, calm and quiet. Billy Dewitt had slept deeply the night before in the first bed he had occupied for many weeks, courtesy of Laredo. There had been no shooting in the streets to indicate that Jake Worthy might have been found. The truth was probably that, despite the rabid intentions of the posse, most of them were still dog-tired as well and had quickly abandoned their search for the bank robber after a few stops in the local saloons.

There was a rap at the door and Billy's nerves jumped, but the familiar voice called, 'Billy, can I come in?'

'Sure, Riley, I'm awake.'

Morning sunlight shafted through the sheer blue curtains hanging on the windows. Distantly a dog barked and someone yelled at someone else.

Ellis, Arizona was waking up, if slowly. Laredo was a surprise to see. He'd had a fresh shave. His jeans were washed, his dark-red shirt seeming store-clean, his dusty, fawn-colored Stetson now clean and blocked. Billy Dewitt stepped into his trail-dirty jeans, feeling slightly ashamed.

'How did you do that?' Billy asked, nodding at Laredo's clothes. 'Get cleaned up?'

'The hotel sent my things out last night and delivered them this morning,' Laredo said, sitting in a wooden chair near the window where he could catch the cool breeze. 'If I'd known you needed some help, I would have said something.'

'I guess I didn't know hotels did such things for a man. I haven't spent much time in them. I suppose you have.'

'Too much time,' Laredo said with a distant smile.

'What now?' Billy asked, flipping his

gunbelt around his waist, reaching for his hat.

'I already told you that we need to talk to the local law. If any shooting does start I'd like them to know what side we're on. First, though, let's have ourselves a real breakfast.'

They walked down the uncarpeted stairs to the hotel lobby. There was a restaurant attached to the hotel and to reach it they passed through an arched entranceway beside the hotel desk. Inside the airy restaurant were nine or ten scattered round tables. Along one wall ran a long bench table for larger parties. All were covered with clean red-and-white-checked cloths. Laredo inclined his head toward a table sitting in a corner with four round-back chairs arranged around it.

It was well away from the doors and windows, Billy noticed. Laredo, it seemed, was always working — whether it showed or not. As expected, Laredo took the chair with its back to the wall. Billy sat and began looking for a waitress.

One was not long in arriving. A young woman, she was, still in her teens, with dark, slightly-disordered hair and a full mouth attempting to smile its way into a new day which would be filled with hard work, rude comments and demanding customers — all of which were supposed to be handled with good humor in her business. She wasn't quite up to form yet.

Laredo asked for a pot of coffee and said they'd be ready to order in a few minutes.

'Are those fresh biscuits I smell?' Billy asked.

'They are,' the girl answered. 'And we've honey to go with them this morning.' Her smile brightened a little as she answered Billy Dewitt. Billy watched as the petite waitress walked away, swaying slightly.

'I think she likes you,' Laredo said.

'Do you . . . ? Ah, hell, Laredo, you know it's her job to smile,' Billy said sheepishly.

'Could be,' Laredo said. They waited

until the waitress came back with their coffee pot and two white ceramic mugs. She was also carrying a plate with four biscuits and a glass jar containing honey.

'I thought you'd be wanting these,' she said, speaking only to Billy.

'I do, thank you.' He glanced at Laredo. 'Are we ready to order yet?'

'Go ahead,' Laredo answered, pouring their coffee. 'Just get me whatever you're having.'

What Billy was having was four fried eggs, ham and hotcakes with strawberry preserves. The girl scribbled the order down on her pad as if with pleasure. When she left this time, it was with a lingering smile.

Laredo said, 'Yes, I'm pretty sure she likes you.' He took a sip of his strong black coffee while Billy split and buttered a roll.

The kid said, 'I sure wish you'd told me how I could've got my clothes cleaned.' He was still looking wistfully after the girl, who had vanished into the kitchen. 'I must look a mess.'

'You can spruce up and come back for supper,' Laredo told him. 'We'll still be in Ellis come sundown.'

'Ah, she'll probably be off work by then.'

'Better yet,' Laredo said and Billy just stared at him, then fell off into his private thoughts.

With breakfast finished, Laredo led a lagging Billy out into the bright morning sunshine. Laredo stopped the first man they met. 'Can you tell us where we can find the law in this town?'

'You mean we have some in Ellis?' the stranger answered with a laugh. 'If you mean Marshal Hicks, he's probably taking his morning nap in his office. That's three blocks down on the other side of the street.'

'He didn't seem too favorably impressed with this Marshal Hicks,' Billy said, as they made their way across the dusty street.

'There's always someone who doesn't like the local law,' Laredo replied.

'I suppose. Look, Riley!' Billy called, pointing down the street. Laredo only nodded. He had already caught sight of David Bean and Lester Burnett hanging around the front door of a saloon which seemed not to have opened its doors yet. A small crowd of impatient drinkers waited with them at the entrance for the bartender to swing open the gate to paradise.

'They haven't found Jake Worthy yet,' Laredo said.

'Maybe they're just filling up with whiskey in case they happen to stumble across him,' Billy said. 'I can't see either of those two going up against a man like Jake Worthy sober.'

'No,' Laredo believed. 'They'll just stay around close enough to Goodnight to be able to swoop down wanting their share.'

The door to the marshal's office was peeling red. It stood open at this morning hour. Laredo and Billy stepped in and stood exchanging looks with a youngish-looking man with red hair and a sweeping mustache. His hair was neatly parted and slicked down with pomade. He wore gold-rimmed spectacles. Laredo would not have taken him for a lawman, but he occupied the chair behind the marshal's desk. In the far corner of the timbered room a man of some physical substance wearing a twill town suit stood looking through a stack of what seemed to be Wanted posters. His head was squarish, his nose flared widely across his face. He had a stare for Laredo which seemed accusing.

'Marshal Hicks?' Laredo asked, looking from one man to the other.

'I'm Hicks,' the narrow man behind the desk said, sitting up a little straighter. 'What can I do for you?'

'It'll take a while to explain,' Laredo said, walking toward the desk. Billy lingered near the door, hat in hands.

'I've got the time; have a seat,' the marshal said, toeing a chair out for Laredo to sit on.

'There was a bank robbery over in Quirt,' Laredo began.

'A bank? When was this?' the bulky man asked, looking rattled.

'Last week,' Laredo told him. The marshal was smiling when Laredo looked back.

'Mr Dodd here runs the Bank of Ellis,' the marshal told Laredo. 'He gets a little nervous when he hears about robberies.'

'Yes, and I have every right to,' Dodd said with heat. 'That's why I come in here so often. I go over every Wanted poster the marshal is sent,' he told Laredo, 'although no one else seems to. I want to mark these men's descriptions in my memory.'

'A wise precaution,' Laredo said expressionlessly.

'Now, then,' the marshal said. 'You were saying . . . '

'I was with a posse riding after this bank robber led by Sheriff Fowler, you probably know him.'

'Fowler? Oh, yes,' the marshal said, scratching at his narrow chin. 'I know Fowler. He's a good man.'

'When we hit the county line down at Yavapai Creek, Fowler turned back, not wanting to cross it.'

'But you came ahead?' Hicks asked, leaning forward, his eyes intent.

'The entire posse did. Fowler cautioned them that they have no mandate on this side of the river, but they decided to pursue the bank robber on their own.'

'Well, I can see that they might have a powerful wish for revenge against the man who'd robbed their bank,' Hicks said, his fingers working their way up from his chin to scratch at his scalp.

'Who's the bank robber?' Dodd asked excitedly. 'Is he here now, in Ellis? Do you think he'll strike again?'

'The bank robber's name is Jake Worthy,' Laredo told him.

'And he's here! The bank robber?' Dodd nearly shouted, approaching the marshal's desk.

Both Laredo and Hicks ignored the nervous banker.

'Jake Worthy was last seen riding a

buckskin horse with a splash of white on its chest, though he may have switched to a three-year-old sorrel by now.' Laredo then verbally sketched a description of Worthy for the marshal. 'The posse members believe Worthy will be resting up in Ellis after the long trail. They mean to capture him if they can.'

'All right, you're telling me that I have a band of well-meaning vigilantes in town,' Hicks said with a frown.

'I am. I can give you their names if it's of any help.'

'Help to do what? What do you expect me to do to, or with, these men? Come to think of it, who are you and what are you doing here?' The marshal's eyes narrowed slightly behind the lenses of his round spectacles.

'I was with the posse by chance. The bank happened to be robbed while I was staying over in Quirt.' Billy saw Laredo reach into his shirt and remove a flat, tightly folded document in a leather wallet. 'Here are my credentials.'

Hicks took the folded paper and read it slowly, carefully. The seal of the territory of Arizona was embossed at the head, as Billy could see from his distance, but Marshal Hicks seemed dubious for some reason. He let the document flutter to his desk and Laredo picked it up, replacing it in the leather wallet.

'That gives you pretty wide-spreading authorization, doesn't it?' Hicks said. 'Something like a Territorial Marshal.'

'Not quite,' Laredo said. 'I haven't any authority to arrest a man.'

'Just to retrieve the stolen funds.'

'Yes. That's the sticky part. The new legislature is being lobbied to change the wording of the legal statute, but for now I am the man the Territorial Bank Examiner authorizes to recover any stolen funds. By any means necessary.'

'I don't think I've ever had an occasion to run into one of your sort before,' Hicks said with a following yawn.

'Then you've done your job. You've never had a bank robbery,' Laredo said with a smile in Dodd's direction.

'Who's the kid over there?' Hicks asked as if he had noticed Billy Dewitt for the first time.

'He's with me, sort-of my apprentice,' Laredo lied glibly.

'Training him to replace you when you retire, are you?' Hicks asked.

Laredo told the marshal soberly, 'Retirement can come unexpectedly in my profession.'

'I suppose.' Hicks rose and walked to the iron stove in the corner. 'Either of you want some coffee?'

Laredo and Billy both declined. The banker, Dodd, had started toward the door. 'Time for me to get to work. I'll see you soon, Hicks. Please let me know if you get any new Wanted posters in.'

'I'll do that, Dodd,' Hicks said with an indifferent wave of his hand. When the door had closed behind Dodd, Hicks walked back to his chair, tin cup of coffee in his hand. 'Most nervous man I ever did meet.'

'It's a big responsibility he has.'

'Sure. Now back to your situation,' Hicks said, seating himself. 'What you have done, you are telling me, is bring a lot of trouble to my little town.'

Ruffled slightly by the marshal's tone, Laredo said, 'It was already here. I just want to clean it up as bloodlessly as possible.'

'It's your idea to find Jake Worthy and retake the bank loot before these other men can do it.'

'That's about it.'

'Think pretty highly of yourself, don't you?' Hicks asked in a tone that again rankled Laredo.

'Well, I've been fortunate enough to have succeeded before,' he answered.

'I suppose you must have,' Hicks allowed, 'or they wouldn't still have you working for them.' He sipped at the hot coffee. 'All right. I'll leave you to your work. Unless Worthy pops his head up. I'd have to arrest him on sight. Or if these others from the posse start any trouble in Ellis — then I'll take them in as well. Any of them I have to be particularly careful with?'

'Jesse Goodnight,' Billy Dewitt put in. It was the first time he had spoken to the marshal, figuring it was Laredo's job to do so.

Hicks's eyes flickered toward Billy. Then he asked, 'I think I know that name from a while ago. Wasn't he — ?'

'He was arrested and convicted of manslaughter about five years ago for the killing of a gambler named Adonis Klotz.'

Hicks nodded. 'I remember that case; not well, but I heard something about it. Stuck in my mind because of the names. Goodnight and Adonis. And Klotz!' Hicks smiled but Laredo didn't.

'Well, Jesse Goodnight is here. He's the leader of the vigilantes.'

'I see. He'll bear watching, won't he? Once a killer . . . '

'He'll bear watching,' Laredo agreed. 'If the others came to Ellis hoping only to get rich on stolen money Jesse Goodnight has come here to do murder.'

6

Marshal Hicks sat silently sipping his coffee while Laredo ran down the rest of what he knew — holding back only what he now suspected. He explained about Jake Worthy's failure to provide Jesse Goodnight with an alibi when Goodnight shot the gambler, and Goodnight's conviction that it was because they were both interested in the same woman in Quirt.

'Toss over your pal for a skirt, huh?' Hicks murmured in a way that would have been an insult to all involved had they been there.

'Anyway,' Laredo went on, ignoring the marshal's comment, 'it seems that Jake Worthy knew where to find Bonnie Sue Garret and he rode there.'

'We have a party named Garret living in one of the little cottages out in Beacon Valley.'

'That would be Bonnie Sue's aunt. The posse escorted Bonnie Sue there after we found her alone in the wild country.'

'Mighty Christian of you,' Hicks cracked.

'The woman hadn't done anything. Besides, she gave us an assumed name.'

'Rita Poole,' Billy said.

'Never heard that name around here,' Marshal Hicks said. Then he asked, 'If Worthy went by to meet the woman, why didn't he take her with him?'

'He might have figured that she would slow him down or maybe he was tired of her. More likely he didn't feel like sharing the money. I believe he took her horse not because he needed it but to keep her from following him.'

'Then Goodnight shows up?' Hicks asked, almost with marvel. 'What a lucky woman.'

'That must be what she was thinking when she saw him. And Goodnight now figures he has won back his old love. I'm sure that's the way Bonnie Sue would play it up. Especially now that she sees Goodnight as having a better hand to play than Jake Worthy.'

'Because of the extra posse men?'

'Yes. He's pretty sure now that he has Worthy cornered in this town somewhere, and he means to have the money and have his blood. And Bonnie Sue. All debts paid, Bonnie Sue his pretty little woman again.'

'Yes, I'd like to hear the encouragement Bonnie Sue was giving him.'

'Jesse Goodnight doesn't need much in the way of encouragement. She's playing up to him, naturally; it's a way for her to win in the game too.'

'Kind-of a nasty little bunch, aren't they?' Hicks said, his eyes meeting Laredo's for the first time in a long time.

'They are; let's see if we can't do something to end it. I guarantee you Goodnight and the posse are out now searching for Jake Worthy.'

'Unless he's hiding out . . . '

Hicks stopped. Laredo prodded him: 'What were you going to say?'

'Just thinking,' the marshal said. 'Suppose Worthy feels cornered, which he is, who could he rely on to shelter him? Maybe little Bonnie Sue.'

'You mean she is playing both sides of the street?' Billy asked in amazement.

'Why not?' Hicks asked. 'She seems to have gotten away with it up to this point, and the girl doesn't seem to mind who it is that butters her bread.'

'Do you think that Marshal Hicks's hunch could be right?' Billy asked, as the two men stepped out into the narrow band of shade cast by the awning overhanging the marshal's office. 'Could Worthy be at the Garret place?'

'I don't think Jake Worthy would move that fast; I don't think he's scared enough yet to convince himself that Bonnie Sue's protection is worth a cut of the loot.'

'Or that she would deal straight with him — not sneaking off to inform Goodnight where he was holed up.'

Laredo nodded. 'There's that — Worthy knows what sort of woman he's dealing with by now. Maybe because she overplayed her hand back at her own house. She might have even made a grab for the money while he slept. She did something, said something, because since Worthy rode there, he did have something in mind concerning the woman when he first made that decision. Something changed his mind. Who knows what. Maybe he just got smart and saw her a little clearer. I know that if I were ever to go out with Bonnie Sue Garret, I'd be sure to have my pockets sewn up first.'

'She's pretty,' Billy mused, as they stepped down to again cross the dusty street.

'Bonnie Sue Garret is too pretty. She knows that she attracts men and they'll do anything for her. That's probably what her entire life has been based on.'

'I wasn't talking about Bonnie Sue Garret,' Billy said, nodding toward the pretty little waitress who was standing at the window of a millinery shop, wistfully studying the window display.

'There's all kinds, aren't there, Laredo.'

'All kinds,' Laredo said, thinking of his own Dusty, who waited for him down in Crater where he had been headed before this business with Jake Worthy came up, and where he was returning as soon as it was ended.

'They're still there,' Billy said, nudging Laredo as they sauntered in the direction of the saloon. In front of the batwing doors David Bean and Lester Burnett stood with mugs of beer, watching passing faces.

'I sort-of doubt that's what Jesse meant when he told them to look around the local saloons for Jake Worthy,' Laredo commented.

'Where do you think Goodnight is?' Billy asked.

'There's no telling, but he'll be working harder than these two. Every hotel and flophouse, barbershop, every place a man can catch a meal, all the gunshops, tailors . . . Goodnight will have been there.'

'I wonder if they found that buckskin

horse Jake Worthy was riding — or the sorrel Bonnie Sue says he stole from her.'

'Do you?' Laredo asked with a hidden smile of approval.

'Sure, because if they have I'd surely have one of my men watching those animals instead of hanging around a saloon. If they haven't — well, why is that? Is Jake Worthy gone again?'

'You're thinking right,' Laredo told him. 'There may be no benefit in it for us, but suppose we start by asking around at all the stables. You're right — either Worthy's horse is here and merits watching, or it's gone, and we need to know where.'

'It could be picketed out anywhere,' Billy said as they walked on. 'But he'd need to have it close by in case the net tightened up around him.'

'I agree with you again. Somewhere close but sheltered. After we check the stables, we'll start using our imagination and poking around some.'

'I wish we could be sure that it's not

hidden out on the Garret property.'

'We'll find out,' Laredo believed, and now Billy turned his head and saw Marshal Hicks stepping out of his office to swing into the saddle of a blotchy-looking paint pony hitched at the rail.

'Do you think he's riding out to the Garret place?' Billy asked.

'I do,' Laredo answered. 'He was sort-of wedded to the theory that Worthy would be hiding out there.'

'You don't believe it?' Billy inquired as they halted in front of a tall, double-doored stable.

'I don't know,' Laredo said. 'I sort-of doubt it, but I guessed that the marshal would check that out for us.'

'You're letting the marshal do a part of your work?' Billy asked in amazement.

Laredo's face was almost straight when he replied, 'It's his job, too, wouldn't you say?' He placed a hand on Billy's shoulder, turning him. 'Come on, let's go look at some ponies.'

Inside they met a dumpy little man in

faded overalls. He had an unmanaged bushy mustache that sprouted in all directions. His face was pocked, his mouth pursed with an unhappiness that was probably perpetual.

When they asked him a question he exploded with the anger that seemed typical of all unimportant men when they are braced in their own small kingdoms.

'How many more men are going to come by asking about that horse?' he erupted, after Laredo had asked his question.

'Sorry,' Laredo said soothingly. 'Are you saying other men have been here, looking for the buckskin?'

'That's what I mean,' the stablehand said, wiping his hands on a red rag. 'It must be a mighty important horse — it or its rider. Stolen, is it?' he asked, his harsh voice smoothing slightly. 'Or is the man riding it an outlaw?'

Laredo declined to answer the man, angering him again. After glancing along the rows of horses sheltered in the stable, Billy and Laredo went out onto the heated street again. A pair of mounted cowboys dragged past, stirring up the fine white dust. Billy's eyes continued to search the street eagerly.

'She's probably back to work by now,' Laredo said, not needing to be a mind-reader to know who Billy Dewitt was searching for. 'Keep your eyes open for Jake Worthy and Jesse Goodnight — I don't know which one is more dangerous right now.'

'I've never seen Jake Worthy . . . ' Billy started to say, 'but talk about dangerous ones! Look there, Laredo.'

Laredo's eyes were attracted to a one-horse carriage trotting toward them from the end of the street. Rita Poole — Bonnie Sue Garret — was driving it, sitting upright and looking proud of herself in her yellow dress and wide white hat.

'What do you make of that?' Billy asked, as the carriage horse trotted briskly past them.

'I can't make anything of it, and she's

not going to tell us what she's up to.' Laredo leaned up against the wooden wall of a dry goods store. 'Let's just wait a minute and see where she goes.'

Where she went was a little surprising. She drew her rig up directly in front of the stable they had just exited. In a minute they could see her talking to the stablehand. Only now the sour, glowering stablehand was smiling so wide it must have hurt his face. He bowed in an obliging way, seeming to be promising his best services.

'She just knocks men down like ninepins, doesn't she?' Billy said.

'It's her life's work and she's very good at it,' Laredo replied, as they watched Bonnie Sue walk across the street, twirling a yellow parasol.

'She's a dangerous package.'

'Something Jake Worthy may have come to realize,' Laredo said.

'But what about Jesse Goodnight?'

'Goodnight has just finished up five years in prison,' Laredo commented. 'Talk about giving Bonnie Sue a running start at her prey.'

They watched her enter the same millinery shop where they had earlier seen the waitress looking in the window. When Bonnie Sue was gone, Laredo nudged Billy. 'Come on, I doubt there's anything to be learned by watching a woman shop.'

They made their way along the heated street to the next stable in town, the one across from the hotel where they had put up their own horses. The stablehand with the long white beard recognized them.

'Riding out, gentlemen?' he asked, leaning on his rake.

'Not just now,' Laredo said. 'We were just looking for a friend that might have ridden in.' He described Worthy and the buckskin horse.

The bearded man shook his head. 'No one like that. You're not the first ones to ask, though. The man must have a lot of friends.'

'He's pretty well known,' Laredo agreed. 'Tell me, are there any more stables in town or folks with horse pens nearby who might pasture his pony out for him?'

The old man scratched his head. 'There's a few. Jennings down south has been known to take in a horse now and then. Rates are cheap, but he's a mile or so out of town, so most folks find it kind-of inconvenient.'

'Anyone else?' Billy Dewitt asked.

'There's folks who would be glad to do it for someone they knew, but not as a commercial venture. Does your friend have any family or friends in the area?'

'Not that I know of,' Laredo answered. 'Thanks for your time.'

Outside, away from the vexing horseflies, Billy said, 'Maybe Marshal Hicks was right — if Worthy is in town those horses either disappeared or they're out at Bonnie Sue's place.'

'You're right,' Laredo agreed, crossing the street again toward the hotel. The street was now bustling with pedestrians, dawdling cowboys and wagons crowding the avenue.

'You do think that Hicks was on the right trail, then?' Billy asked. They had achieved the plankwalk in front of the hotel. Laredo removed his hat, wiped out the sweat band with his scarf and repositioned it.

'No. I think you're right about Worthy's horses. You said they had either disappeared or were out at the Garret place. I think they've disappeared.'

Billy gave Laredo another of his puzzled looks.

Laredo explained: 'Think about it. Jake Worthy is not short on brains. He knows that one way he can be identified is by the horse he rides. He probably got rid of that buckskin. Gave it away, sold it. It wouldn't matter to him which. He has plenty of money to buy another horse when he needs it. The sorrel he never wanted anyway, he just didn't want Bonnie Sue following him on it. I'd say some saddle tramp or man stranded and afoot got the bargain of his life from Jake Worthy.'

'Both horses are long gone?'

'I'd say so. I could be wrong, but if I were Worthy and had the money to replace my horse, I'd get rid of that one as soon as I could.'

'But you think Worthy is still in town?'

Laredo shook his head. 'That's the difficult part to figure. He had a night to rest up and eat, to outfit himself. If he bought another horse, he could be riding miles away from Ellis, and us with no way of knowing which way he's gone.'

'I suppose you're right,' Billy said. 'We should have been asking about a man who bought a new horse and not somebody who had left his to be cared for.'

'It would have been a better idea,' Laredo agreed. 'But how many horses do you think change hands in a day around here — through a sale, a trade, a wager?'

'A lot if it's like most places I've been,' Billy said. His expression now was crestfallen, defeated.

'Cheer up, Billy,' Laredo said, 'I think Jake Worthy is still in town even though that's just a feeling.'

'Why would he stay around? He knows he could shake us off his trail now.'

'How could he shake Jesse Goodnight — ever? Jesse wants Worthy's blood and he won't quit hunting the man. By now Jake Worthy must surely have seen Jesse around town or at least heard the description of a man asking about him,' Laredo said. 'Maybe Jake Worthy has decided to stay long enough to finish matters off here and now. One back shot in some alley would remove the weight of Jessie Goodnight from his mind for ever.'

'But if Worthy got caught,' Billy objected, 'he'd be strung up and all of it will have been for nothing.'

Laredo nodded his agreement. Both men stepped aside to let a pair of well-dressed town ladies pass them on the boardwalk. When the women were out of earshot, Laredo went on: 'We are agreed that Worthy is canny, sly. We know he's well-heeled now, traveling with gold in his poke. If he wants to have things finished, Billy, there's no reason in the world for him to do it himself.'

'Hired guns?'

'Why not? He sees himself as outnumbered five-to-one now. I don't doubt he is capable of hiring some guns. How many men do you think could be picked up in a saloon — men down on their luck, men who lost the game when the last card was turned over, even drunks looking at the bottom of their last bottle — by a man whose pockets are filled with money?'

'More than a few,' Billy answered, frowning. 'But, Laredo, if you happen to be right, have you thought that maybe Worthy's thinking wouldn't end with removing Goodnight from his trail? He could hire men to be put on to us as well.'

'Yes, I have considered that, Billy. We

won't know until it's too late, but I think we should walk warily in Ellis from here on, because we may already have bull's eyes painted on our backs.'

7

The young waitress's name was Nan Singleton. Billy found this out when they returned to the hotel restaurant at noon. Uncertainly, shyly, he had asked the older blonde woman who served them about her when he did not see her working.

'Ah, honey,' the waitress said, placing coffee cups down between Billy and Laredo. 'You mean little Nan. Nan Singleton. She works what we call a split-shift: breakfast and supper, that is. She's off during the middle of the day, but she doesn't seem to mind, says she has more time to get her chores done. Me, it would drive crazy . . . '

The waitress went on to express more of her personal preferences and tell them some of her own problems, but neither man was listening. Laredo, who had removed his hat and combed back his copper-colored hair with his fingers, sat smiling vacantly at her, nodding at intervals until the waitress was summoned to another table.

'Well,' Laredo said, folding his hands together on the table, 'you've got her name now.'

'Yes. I don't know what good it does me. Everybody else who comes in here probably knows her name anyway.'

'Probably.'

'I wish I knew where she lived, Laredo.'

'Ask the waitress when she comes back,' Laredo prompted. 'If she doesn't want to tell you, it should be easy to find out. Nan Singleton lives in this town, works in this restaurant. People know her. We can ask around. I guarantee she'll be easier to find than Jake Worthy.'

That brought Billy back to the real world. Men maybe out looking for a chance to gun them down, Goodnight on a rampage, the marshal gone, Bonnie Sue frittering the day away in a shop, Worthy keeping his head down in some nearby hide-out . . .

'We sure walked ourselves into something, didn't we?' Billy muttered, refilling his coffee cup.

'I'm kind-of used to it,' Laredo answered. 'It goes with the territory, as they say.' After a thoughtful pause, Laredo told the blond kid, 'You know, Billy, you've got no sort of obligation to stay around here if you want to leave.'

'Thanks, Laredo. I know that, but I sure want to be around to see how it plays out.'

Laredo smiled, nodded and studied Billy Dewitt's face. He wanted to see how matters evolved, sure. Also, Laredo thought, he wasn't ready to just ride away and leave Nan Singleton behind yet.

Well, let the kid have his dreams. Laredo himself was looking over the men in the restaurant, looking for a man sitting alone, a left-handed man with black eyes who formerly wore a black mustache, for Laredo was certain that by now Jake Worthy would have gotten himself shaved clean as a sort of disguise. He would have to remind Billy that Worthy's gun would be slung on his left hip — unless Worthy was also willing to wear it on his unaccustomed right side to throw people off. That seemed unlikely; Jake Worthy figured to need that gun before he left Ellis, and he would need it quickly if he happened to run into Jesse Goodnight.

And where was Goodnight? They had not seen him this morning although his henchmen and former posse partners had been easy enough to find. Bean and Lester Burnett seemed to have given up all pretense of searching for Worthy after one rapid, desultory sweep through the town.

Probably they were right — Jake Worthy was not going to be found walking the streets at high noon. That would not stop Jesse Goodnight. He would be peeking into dustbins, prodding piles of refuse, scrounging through the alleys and flophouses looking for the face of the man who had doomed him to five years in prison. He would not quit.

Where, then, was Jake Worthy? He was well and completely hidden in town or nearby. At the Garret place? Laredo did not think so, but he had been wrong before. If he was, he was going to meet Marshal Hicks shortly. It could be that Hicks would catch Worthy by surprise and that would be the end of it.

Again, Laredo doubted it. Worthy was just too savvy, too clever to be taken unaware. Bonnie Sue was in Ellis shopping as if she did not have a care in the world or a bandit hiding in her house. And she had the money to go shopping. Whose?

Laredo thought fleetingly of the old woman out at the cottage. Laredo figured her for the sort of old lady who would simply put up with whatever came her way without complaint. Once before he had made that sort of judgment only to have an old, harmless-looking soul break out a shotgun from her closet when she'd had enough.

'Got it all figured out?' Billy asked.

'What's that?' Laredo asked.

'I never saw a man eat an entire meal without a word,' Billy Dewitt said with a smile, and Laredo noticed that his plate was indeed empty. He had been thinking while he ate and eating while he thought. Now he was out of both food and thoughts.

'Was it any good?' Laredo asked.

'Pork roast, mashed potatoes and corn on cob,' Billy told him. 'Mighty good. What do we do now?'

'I wish I knew. If you want to go asking around about Nan Singleton, go ahead. Take the afternoon off.'

'No, sir! Not if you need me.'

'That's just the thing. I don't know what I'd need you for. I seem to have reached the end of my road. I'm afraid I'm just going to have to sit back and wait for whatever it is that's going to happen.'

'Laredo,' Billy had gotten to his feet and was now hovering over the table, an earnest expression on his young face, 'what you said to me goes for you, too. We could both just saddle up and ride out of Ellis.'

Laredo shook his head. 'Not me. It's my job, Billy. It's what they pay me for.'

'There must have been times when you . . . failed before.'

'Yes, and I remember every one of them bitterly. I'm not going to let this job turn out to be another one. Jake Worthy is so near I can almost smell him, and he has something I am sworn to recover.'

Stepping out onto the plankwalk once more, Billy, with a toothpick in his lips, began to speak. 'You know, Laredo, I think that I'll — '

That was as far as he got before a rifle opened up from the roof of the building across the street. Three shots thudded into the siding of the hotel while a fourth shattered one of the painted front windows. Laredo threw himself against Billy's knees, rolling the kid down while his eyes searched for a target on the far side of the street.

Laredo got to one knee, his Colt in his hand, but there was not even a trailing wisp of smoke to be seen seconds after the shooting.

Men along the street had scattered for shelter when the shots rang out. Now they tentatively emerged from cover, most with pistols in hand, looking around and up and asking one another where the shots had come from and what it was about.

Laredo thought he knew.

'Are we going after him?' Billy asked. His eyes were wide. He had lost his hat and his blond hair hung across his forehead. He looked very young and quite fearful.

Laredo shook his head. 'He'd be long gone by the time we could get over there and find our way to the roof.'

'Was it Jake Worthy?' Billy asked, snatching up his hat, taking Laredo's hand to be tugged upright.

'Doubt it. I think it was someone he sent out, though. A man who didn't quite earn his wages.'

'Think there will be others?' Billy asked, dusting his elbows off.

'If there was one, others will be sent until someone does the job right.'

'I've got to say, that surprised me,' Billy said, his voice still a little shaky.

'Me too,' Laredo replied. 'I didn't think we'd see anyone crawling out of their hiding places before dark. I suppose this one was eager to win whatever bonus they've been promised. He took a chance at midday.'

A man wearing an apron and another in a blue town suit had emerged from the restaurant now that it seemed safe outside. The man in the suit stood in front of the broken glass which now read 'RANT' in large red letters, holding his hand to his head. Laredo heard a bit of the complaint.

' . . . from Tucson! Know how long it will take . . . a painter . . . '

Some of the restaurant workers and a few of the customers had come out of the restaurant now to survey the damage. Among them, straining to peer over a man's shoulder was the diminutive Nan Singleton, still in her street clothes. Laredo didn't have to call attention to her. Billy had noticed her. He smiled shyly; she frowned.

'She thinks it is our fault,' Billy said. Laredo looked that way again to see that the small, dark-haired girl had slipped away into the building.

'Well, I suppose it is in a way, don't you?'

'Hell of a thing, blaming the victims for the crime,' Billy mumbled, as if he had discovered a flaw in Nan's character. 'Laredo,' — Billy had given up calling him Riley — 'how did he even know who we were, that we were looking for Jake Worthy?'

'We've made no secret of it. We've been asking around. We've visited the marshal's office as well. It doesn't take a genius to figure out we're looking for Worthy. Which leads me to another thought — we've got to tell Bean and Burnett that they're running a risk in Ellis.'

'They must already know that,' Billy Dewitt said, his voice cool. 'Besides, that's Jesse Goodnight's job.'

'I don't think Goodnight cares if they live or die — they might draw Worthy out into the open for him.'

'You care about them?' Billy asked.

'Not a lot, but they are men and I don't want to see them killed, do you?'

'No, of course not,' Billy answered, though he did so with a sigh of discontent. Neither the dirt farmer nor the Quirt big-shot had done much to endear themselves and, by tracking with Jesse Goodnight, they had revealed their character plainly. They were looking to make some money from the death or capture of Jake Worthy.

'Let's take a walk,' Laredo suggested, and he started along the plankwalk, heading west again toward the saloon where they had seen Bean and Burnett earlier. 'Keep your eyes open,' Laredo warned needlessly.

'From now on I'm all eyes,' Billy Dewitt said.

'Here comes the man,' Laredo said after they had walked a block and a half. Billy looked back down the street to see Marshal Hicks riding into town on his tired-appearing paint pony. 'Step back into this alley while he goes by.'

Billy looked a question at Laredo as they entered the half-shaded alley cluttered with empty nail kegs and broken crates. 'When he hears what happened, Hicks will be wanting to have a talk with us. I'd rather have it later than now,' Laredo said in a low voice as they watched Hicks trail past.

'You figure he'll blame us too?' Billy asked. Laredo nodded his head. 'Well,' Billy said with more enthusiasm, 'at least we now know for sure that Jake Worthy isn't hiding out at the Garret place.'

'No,' Laredo corrected. 'We know that Hicks didn't find him there.' He nodded his head again and the two men walked the rest of the way to the saloon, which seemed to be picking up a head of celebratory steam now. Men jeered, shouted and cursed inside. On the plankwalk, half a dozen men still loitered, holding mugs and at least one whiskey bottle in their hands. Eyes raked and evaluated Laredo and Billy as they approached the batwing doors, but no word was said as the two strangers elbowed their way into the saloon.

'Do you see them?' Laredo asked.

'No, maybe they went . . . hold it — that's Bean, isn't it?'

And it was David Bean, standing at the end of the bar as if he needed it to prop him up. Apparently he had switched from beer to something stronger, and the farmer, who could have had little time to waste in saloons back in Quirt or enough money to do damage to himself with drink, was more than a little intoxicated now. On Goodnight's money? Jesse Goodnight would not be appreciative if so. Goodnight had earned whatever money he had by laboring for five years on a prison rock pile.

'We'd better have a chat with him,' Laredo said. 'Do you see Lester Burnett around anywhere?'

'No. Maybe he's actually trying to get some work done.'

'Could be. He's more than a little terrified of Goodnight.'

Reaching Bean, they managed to elbow up to the scarred bar on either side of him.

'How's everything going, Bean?' Laredo asked quietly. Bean's hand stopped in mid-motion, his jaw dropped and his eyes went nearly as wide as saucers. Maybe he thought Goodnight had caught him loafing on the job. He glanced at Laredo and then at Billy.

'Oh, it's you two,' Bean said. His voice was slurred, hesitant in forming words. Laredo had to strain to comprehend the man's drunken speech. 'What are you still doing here?'

'Waiting for Jake Worthy to pop up,' Laredo said, smiling.

'Well you can forget all about that!' Bean said. The farmer staggered a little, his planted elbows sliding along the bar. If Billy had not been there to bookend him, Laredo thought the farmer might have toppled over to the floor. 'The money is ours,' Bean said, with a damp hiss that reeked of raw whiskey.

'Who says?' Laredo asked.

Bean stuttered his way to an answer. 'We do. Jesse Goodnight does. You two had better make up your minds that there is no posse any more and you . . . ' he turned on Billy, 'just ride back to Quirt before someone gets hurt.' It was all boozy bluster, of course: David Bean was a small, narrow man. He couldn't have taken Billy Dewitt sober. Laredo maintained his civility with some difficulty.

'That's what we came over here for, Bean,' he said. 'To tell you that someone took a few shots at us, and you and Burnett are in just as much danger as we are.'

'Who . . . says?' Bean demanded, leaving a long gap between the two words. The whiskey-belligerence remained in his eyes. There was no way to speak to the farmer cogently just now.

Billy gave it one last try. 'You'd better watch your back, Bean. Because there are men willing to shoot you wandering this town.'

'Who . . . says?' Bean repeated as if he weren't sure that he had gotten the short sentence out last time.

'The men with the guns say so,' Laredo answered. They might as well finish up quickly here. They had done what they could in the way of warning Bean. 'Where's Burnett?' he asked. Maybe they would have better luck with the townsman.

'Lester . . . ?' Bean looked around the crowded saloon with puzzlement. A light seemed to flicker on in the back of his fuddled skull. 'Oh, I recall!' he said with the triumph of remembering. 'He went over to the stable to see to that white mare of his. You'd think it was his wife, the way he treats it . . . ' Bean's voice trailed off. He might have been trying to make up a joke to go with his remark.

'Let's go, Billy,' Laredo said in the interlude. Bean had lifted a finger as if he had thought of something he wanted to say, but neither Billy nor Laredo wished to stay around and listen to his drunken rambling.

The air outside was heated, but much purer. The white sun beat down on Ellis from almost directly overhead. Glancing that way, Laredo saw the marshal's paint pony standing three-legged in the sun.

'There's one man who doesn't treat his horse like his wife,' Laredo said.

'Maybe. We don't know his wife,' Billy said with a chuckle. Laredo nodded. He didn't know if Hicks had a wife or how he treated her, but he'd bet he didn't leave her standing out, tied to a post in the heat of the day.

'Burnett had his mare at the first stable we visited, didn't he? The one run by the man with the wild mustache and the prickly temper?' Dewitt asked.

'Now, be fair, Billy, he was very nice to Bonnie Sue Garret. But, yes that's where Burnett had his white mare. I saw it.'

'I wonder if Bonnie Sue's rig is still there, or if she went home again,' Billy pondered.

'We'll look. There's no telling. She might have decided to spend the day in Ellis,' Laredo said.

'Why? What could she find to do in this town on an afternoon?'

'Jesse Goodnight is still here. He hasn't seen her properly for five years.'

'You don't believe ... oh, you do believe,' Billy said as they approached the stable. 'That doesn't leave much of a search party left from Goodnight's bunch, does it?'

They found Lester Burnett grooming his white mare. The townsman's suit was torn out at the knees and one elbow by now, his fancy derby hat was dust-yellowed. He looked up sharply as Laredo and Billy Dewitt tramped in.

'You two still here?' he barked.

'That's the way everybody greets us,' Billy said in a low voice.

'Still here,' Laredo told Burnett. 'Though not by much. That's what we came to warn you about. We had a man shoot at us from a rooftop with a rifle. We were just lucky; his shots seemed a little shaky.'

'What's that got to do with me?' Burnett demanded, continuing to brush his mare's flank.

'I hope nothing for your sake,' Laredo told him. With his hat tilted back, Laredo now rested with his forearms on the stall partition and added, 'But it seems logical that anyone wanting me and Billy out of the way will also be wishing to settle his sights on you, Bean and Goodnight.'

'Jake Worthy, you mean,' Burnett said with a flicker of concern passing across his eyes.

'Jake Worthy, I mean. He knows that men have been asking around town about him, and he seems to have a fair idea of who they are and what they're after.'

Lester Burnett cocked his head to

one side and asked, 'Is this really a friendly warning, Riley, or are you trying to convince us to pull out of Ellis and leave Worthy to you?'

'You'll have to decide that for yourself, but if it will help you make up your mind have a look at the front of the hotel restaurant. That's where we were standing when the rifleman made his try.'

'If you go up there,' Billy said, unable to resist a taunt, 'make sure you keep your wits about you while walking the street.' The two left without a goodbye.

'I think he, at least, believes us,' Laredo said as they exited the stable.

'Who cares?' Billy answered shortly. 'Did you see Bonnie Sue's buggy parked out back, and that bay horse she was driving in the back stall?'

'I did,' Laredo answered. 'But right now I — '

His sentence was broken off by the sudden bellow of a heavy handgun from within the stable. There was the roar of the pistol, the following thump of the bullets striking wood and the peculiar high-pitched shriek of a man in mortal terror. Laredo dove for the open door of the stable, shaking his Colt free of its holster as two more shots rang out.

8

'Burnett!' Laredo yelled as he took shelter behind one of the stable stalls' partitions. 'Are you all right?' From the corner of his eye Laredo saw Billy Dewitt easing up beside him, his young face grim. 'Burnett!' Laredo tried again. 'It's Riley!'

'Riley?' Burnett's weakened voice called back. 'I'm hit. I thought it was you who did it.'

'Stay down,' Laredo called back. 'Did you see which way he went?'

'I couldn't see . . . '

Then all three men saw the dark shadow darting toward the side door of the stable, rushing toward the stock pens outside. Laredo went after him, rising to his feet and keeping his head low as he raced in a half-crouch toward the door.

The would-be killer, whoever he was,

was fast on his feet. By the time Laredo reached the door, there was only settling dust to be seen and no indication as to what way the shooter had gone. Laredo crept forward, gun held high as he eased along the peeling, white-painted wall of the stable, eyes squinting against the glare of the midday sun. It was no good, Laredo knew. While he had to inch along, wary of an ambush, the shooter was legging it away at full speed.

He was ready to give it up when he rounded the corner of the stable to find a tall man in a shabby green jacket and flop hat, standing there, holding the lead to a black horse, rifle in his hand.

The stranger had deep-blue eyes set in a face lined by sun and weather. He had a three-day growth of pepper-and-salt whiskers. Tall and angular, the man simply stood his ground and studied Laredo, rifle remaining in his loose grip.

'Finally caught up with us, did you?' Laredo asked and the man's silence only extended itself. The light breeze from the north picked up fine dust and drifted it around them as Billy arrived, breathless and excited. He halted abruptly at the sight of Laredo and the strange rifleman watching each other in tableau.

'Do we want him?' Billy asked hoarsely.

'No,' was Laredo's answer. At that the man with the rifle turned away, leading his horse after him, and vanished up the narrow alley.

'I thought maybe that was Worthy,' Billy said as Laredo turned back toward the stable door, holstering his Colt. 'I've never seen the man, remember.'

'How's Burnett?' Laredo asked.

'I haven't seen him yet but he's well enough to yell and cuss plenty. The little stablehand was checking him over when I came after you.' Billy's curiosity still had not faded. 'That man with the rifle, he's not the one who shot Burnett?'

'No. And before you ask, he's not the one who shot at us at the hotel.'

'Is he someone you know?'

'No,' Laredo answered flatly.

'Someone who knows who you are, then?' Billy wanted to know.

'Not that either,' Laredo said with a hint of impatience.

'Look, if it's none of my business, all right. I thought I had the right to know . . . ' Billy quit talking. They had reached the stall where Lester Burnett sat on the hay-strewn floor, back leaning against a partition. The stable-hand had led the white mare before he tried to tend to Burnett's wound.

Burnett's face was red. He had lost his hat. He was in obvious pain. Looking up, he implored Laredo, 'Get me to a doctor!'

'I'll have you cleaned up quick,' the obnoxious stable man said, his wild mustache twitching with each syllable. 'You won't need no doctor. The bullet that clipped your neck ain't no worse than a shaving nick. The one in your leg went right through. Never caught bone.'

'You don't understand, you madman!' Burnett shouted. The stablehand backed away in a crouch. 'I'm bleeding! I can't move my right leg.' He turned a pleading, pale face — damp with perspiration — toward Laredo. 'I need some decent help.'

Laredo spoke to the stablehand. 'He's never been around guns much. He's a city-squatter.'

'Oh,' the stable man said, satisfied with the explanation.

'Is there a doctor in this town?' Billy Dewitt asked, earning Burnett's gratitude.

'Butcher, I call him. Doc Page. Send for him to patch a bullet hole and you've issued your own death warrant. I say get this man to bed and fill him up with whiskey. He ain't hurt bad. Not for Ellis.'

'Where can we find this Doctor Page?' Billy asked, showing more concern for Burnett's well-being than he probably deserved.

They were given explicit directions

delivered in a rambling monologue. Doc Page was not one of the stablehand's favorite people, for some reason. Between them, Billy and Laredo got Burnett to his feet. It seemed Burnett was about to faint, but he managed to haul himself upright. He looked up at them with haunted, feverish eyes.

'I think he was trying to shoot my mare! Will someone make sure that she's all right?'

'Your horse is fine,' he was told and Burnett nodded his gratitude and allowed himself to be half-carried along out of the stable.

'Sorry,' the townsman managed to mutter to Laredo as he was escorted along the dusty street. 'I should have listened to you when you told me what might happen.'

'It wouldn't have made any difference. Whoever shot you was already in place in the stable by the time we talked to you.'

'I just don't see what they want of me,' Burnett said in a complaining voice as they took him up the steps to the doctor's office.

'Sure you do,' Laredo said. 'They want you to go home, and it's not a bad idea if you ask me.'

★ ★ ★

They left Burnett in the care of a grizzled doctor who must have been nearly eighty years old, and his neat, matronly nurse wearing a clean and ironed white apron. Burnett had become mostly incoherent. All Laredo and Billy could tell the doctor was that someone had plugged him twice with a .44, which the doctor already knew.

Outside the day had grown hotter yet. Few people stirred along the street. Perspiration was whipped off the skin before it could bead. 'The beer must be selling well,' Laredo said.

'Laredo,' Billy Dewitt spoke up. He nodded toward the marshal's office, which was near to both the doctor's office and the stable. 'Hicks was near enough to hear that shooting.'

'He was.'

'Then why . . . ? Let's get something cool to drink,' Billy suggested when it became clear that Laredo wasn't going to answer his unspoken question.

'In there?' Laredo asked as they approached the saloon.

Billy's face took on a sour expression. 'I'd rather find some cool water.'

Laredo nodded. 'So would I.'

The usual knot of men was not crowding the plankwalk near the batwing doors. Perhaps the heat had driven them inside. They were three steps from the doorway when a drunken, staggering, hot-eyed David Bean stumbled and slipped his way out of the saloon.

'You!' the farmer shouted. He had his gun worn around toward the front, his hand resting on its butt. 'I knew you'd come back for me!'

'What the hell are you talking about?' Laredo said quietly. He moved a step away from Billy. Bean might have been a threat to no one but himself just then, but you never knew. More people were shot by fools than marksmen.

'You know what I'm talking about, damn you!' Bean erupted. His hand flinched but did not close around the grips of his pistol. 'I knew you'd come to kill me this morning. But I was too smart to go outside with you. Only thing I regret is telling you where Burnett was, because you just marched over there and shot him down.'

'We didn't shoot him,' Billy tried. Bean's mood was reckless and he had to be calmed down, made to listen to reason. He wasn't yet ready.

'You were seen! Three or four men saw you go into the stable, heard the shots and saw you dragging him out of there, bleeding bad.'

'That's not what happened,' Laredo said, shifting his feet. He did not want to kill Bean, the poor stupid drunk, but it was better than letting Bean shoot him. 'Why would we take Burnett to the doctor's if we wanted him dead?'

'Because you knew you couldn't get

away with it. Too many had seen you go into that stable. Besides, it makes no difference to you if he dies or not — at least he'll be out of the way now.'

'What do you mean, out of the way?' Billy asked. He had taken his hint from Laredo and eased a few paces to one side.

'You know what I mean,' Bean said. He obviously didn't want to mention the stolen money — who knew what other ears were listening? Now David Bean was standing hunched forward, head thrust out, looking like a pale vulture. His eyes were red and glassy. None of this made him any less capable of pulling a trigger.

'All right,' Laredo said, surprising Billy. 'You've got us. Why not march us over to the marshal's office and we'll turn ourselves in?'

'Don't you think I know that you're also in tight with the marshal? Probably offered him a share of — '

'Bean,' Billy said sharply. 'Booze is making you stupid, can't you see that?

There's two of us; you won't get us both and even if you could, the marshal would have you in jail in minutes and you'd never get a chance to spend your share.'

'I'm not falling for any tricks,' Bean said after a moment's hesitation in which he licked his whiskey-dried lips. What was he thinking? Did he believe the story about Lester Burnett, or was he simply playing for a way to get a bigger share of the loot from Goodnight?

It didn't matter: in the next moment the drunken farmer drew his gun. Laredo lurched to one side, Billy ducked and the gun went off close at hand. Bean swayed on his feet for a moment, his eyes going blank. Then he crumpled up like a discarded rag doll. Behind him stood the man who had pulled the trigger.

Neither Laredo not Billy could put a name to the black-bearded man, but he was smiling with pleasure. 'Glad I could be of help, men,' the stranger said. 'I saw he was going to shoot you down and got him first.' Then, still smiling, the man holstered his gun and re-entered the saloon, where a cry of general acclamation went up.

Behind them on the plankwalk, Laredo and Billy Dewitt heard the leather heels of Marshal Hicks's boots racketing on the plankwalk as he rushed toward them. The marshal had his Colt out. His neatly combed hair was not covered by a hat. His spectacles reflected the high sunlight, making blue and gold orbs where his eyes should have been.

'Now what?' Hicks hollered as he halted beside Laredo and Billy. 'You'd better hand over your guns, men.'

They did, just long enough for Hicks to examine them and determine they had not been fired. He looked down at Bean, holstered his weapon and turned the body over to see the farmer's drawn weapon and the .44-sized hole in his back.

'Who did this?' Hicks asked from his crouch.

'Never saw him before. Big man with a full black beard.' Laredo inclined his head toward the saloon doors. 'He went back in there.'

'In there?' There was still a rousing sound of delight echoing within. Hicks blanched. Obviously, the saloon was a place he generally stayed away from. Hicks had a badge on his shirt, but he had little heart to go with it. That much had been obvious to Laredo when the marshal failed to investigate the shooting at the hotel and preferred to simply ignore the ambush of Lester Burnett at the stable. He recalled the comment of the man they had met when they had first arrived in Ellis asking about where they could find the law in the town: 'You mean, we have some in Ellis?'

That man at least had a low impression of Hicks's ability and it seemed to be a generally shared opinion. Certainly no one in the saloon seemed cowed by Hicks's probable appearance. Hicks smoothed down his burnished hair uncomfortably, looked down at the body of Bean again and glanced toward the rowdy saloon. The man was obviously not up to facing an armed killer in his lair.

He asked Laredo imploringly, 'I don't suppose you are supposed to . . . wouldn't . . . ?' Laredo shook his head. He was specifically forbidden by statute from taking part in local law issues which did not involve his directive. Marshal Hicks, who had read Laredo's mandate that very morning, was well aware of that. Laredo was not allowed to risk his prime objective by taking off on tangents, no matter how well meant.

'Well,' Hicks said to Billy, 'you then. You're going to show me the man who did the killing and help me arrest him. You're deputized as of now.'

'I don't even live in Ellis,' Billy pointed out. 'I can't see what this has to do with me.'

'It has plenty to do with you,' Hicks said sharply. 'If I can't find the man you've described, I might have to take a second look at matters. It could turn out that you did the shooting yourself and are trying to shift the blame to an imaginary stranger.'

'You know my gun wasn't even fired!' Billy, who had not had the experience Laredo had with small-town lawmen, was obviously flustered, his face pale, his eyes wide with incomprehension. He looked an appeal at Laredo, who remained silent.

Hicks said, 'That's the way it appears, but it might be I'll have to lock you up for a while until this can be thoroughly investigated.'

Billy let out a small moan. He again looked at Laredo, wondering why the man he thought to be his friend did not step up and object.

'The hell with it,' Billy said with a sigh. 'I'll go with you.'

The glaring expression he settled on Laredo stayed in place as the two 'lawmen' traipsed into the saloon, letting the batwing doors swing shut behind them. Laredo leaned against an awning upright, boot upraised behind him, crossed his arms and waited.

The batwing doors were still fluttering when Hicks's high-pitched voice shouted out, commanding everyone to stay where he was. There was the scraping of table and chair legs on the floor and the sudden roar of a .44 pistol being touched off. Laredo heard a few grunts, the dull thuds of struggle and then the bearded man emerged. Billy Dewitt had hold of the man's belt with his left hand and had the muzzle of his Colt jammed into his ribs. Looking smugly satisfied, Marshal Hicks backed out of the saloon behind them. With a glance at Laredo, Hicks gave an order.

'Walk him to the jailhouse, Dewitt! It's time these loafers and trouble-makers learned their lesson.'

Billy didn't even look Laredo's way as he roughly propelled the man with the beard forward along the plankwalk, marching him toward Hicks's office. Laredo stretched, watched the handful of men who peered out of the saloon after Billy and the marshal, then turned and started up the street toward the restaurant. He still needed that cool water.

The restaurant was virtually empty when Laredo sauntered in and took a seat at his familiar table. The midday crowd had finished with their meal and the supper arrivals hadn't begun to show up yet. Most of them would wait until the sun was lower and the heat of the day had dissipated some before eating.

There was a lone man with a pad and pencil on the table in front of him, dressed in a tradesman's suit, and a lone coffee-drinker sitting staring gloomily at nothing. He looked like a man who might have lost his poke on the last spin of the roulette wheel. There was no need for Laredo to hurry, and so he accepted another glass of cold water from the blonde waitress they had talked to earlier and tried to relax while he devised a plan for himself and Billy once the kid had returned.

He spotted Nan Singleton as she arrived. She looked around the restaurant anxiously, her eyes pausing for a moment at Laredo's table. He nodded at her but the greeting was not returned. Untying her bonnet, Nan scurried into the kitchen.

Laredo had been sitting there for half an hour or so when they came in.

Bonnie Sue Garret clung to the silk-sleeved arm of Jesse Goodnight possessively as they crossed the room.

Her face was flushed, her eyes bright. Goodnight appeared to be proud of himself. They took a table in the center of the restaurant. Both glanced in Laredo's direction at least once, but their expressions were neutral, merely noting his presence.

Laredo watched them for long minutes, trying to guess their intentions. Getting nowhere with that, he gave it up and glanced at the brass-clad octagonal clock on the wall, wondering at Billy's continued absence.

When the kid did arrive minutes

later, Laredo's first inclination was to grin, but he stifled that expression. Billy looked uncomfortable enough sporting the deputy marshal's shield on his shirt. Billy crossed the room, seeming not to have even noticed Bonnie Sue and Goodnight, pulled a chair from the table and sat down, throwing his forearms on the table top.

'Don't you dare laugh, Laredo!' Billy said seriously.

Laredo only shook his head as if with surprise. 'Why would I laugh? Tell me what happened in the saloon and later.'

Billy told his tale, relaxing more as it went along. 'Well, we found Hoop Kingman laughing it up at the bar, regaling men with his tale.'

'Hoop Kingman is . . . ?'

'The man with the beard,' Billy said. 'The man who shot Bean.' Laredo nodded his understanding. 'Marshal Hicks told them all to hold their places, but he was pretty much ignored. I had to punctuate his command by firing a round through the saloon ceiling. That got their attention.'

'It'll do it,' Laredo said.

'Then there was nothing to do but for me to identify Kingman as the gunman. Hicks lifted his pistol, arrested him and gave him to me to escort to the jailhouse.'

'Glad it went smoothly,' Laredo commented. 'I mean, I would have thought the man would put up a fight, this being a murder charge and all.'

'That's what it was, all right, murder for hire. We found fifty gold dollars on him at the jail. They must have come from Jake Worthy. Kingman was a no-account drifter, always broke, according to Hicks.'

'Yes?' Laredo asked, for he knew Billy well enough to know he was not telling something.

'It went well enough,' Billy told him, frowning. 'The reason Kingman didn't give us any trouble or try to get away is that he's claiming self-defense. With me as a witness.'

9

'Self-defense,' Laredo said, nodding. He was vaguely familiar with the territorial statute covering the same.

'Yes,' Billy said with frustration, 'Kingman was laughing as we locked him in a cell, saying he would call me as a witness. It seems that if you're shooting to protect another person's life you are acting in self-defense. Hicks is going to have to consult with the judge, but given the circumstances he thinks Kingman might have a good chance of getting off — '

' — because Bean had his pistol drawn and pointed at us when Kingman shot him.'

'Exactly,' Billy said. 'Kingman says he was trying to keep Bean from doing murder and had every right to shoot him.'

'I don't suppose the court will

consider that Kingman was a gun for hire, paid to shoot anyone associated with Jesse Goodnight.'

'I think that would be a difficult thing to prove, don't you?'

'I do,' Laredo agreed soberly.

'It doesn't look as if Goodnight has gotten the word yet that both of his men are down,' Billy said, nodding toward Jesse Goodnight's table.

'He's been busy,' Laredo guessed. Bonnie Sue and Goodnight had their heads close together, whispering.

'Is it time to eat yet?' Billy asked, suddenly.

'Any time you want,' Laredo answered agreeably. Billy was looking toward the kitchen. Laredo didn't think Billy was waiting so eagerly for food but for the little waitress who might be serving it.

'How about we wait half an hour or so,' Laredo suggested. He studied the young man opposite him. Nothing had been said as yet about the badge Billy was now wearing. There was time. 'There's a razor on my dressing table if you wanted to scrape your face some,' Laredo offered. 'Let's show Nan what you look like all prettied up.'

'Laredo, I . . . ' he began hotly, then his temper cooled off. He was only arguing against himself anyway. As Billy started to rise from his chair, Laredo told him, 'I've heard that a little vinegar will take the tarnish right off that silver shield.'

'I'll try it,' Billy said, absently touching the badge. 'But where . . . ?'

Laredo called the blonde waitress over. Automatically, she reached for her pad and stub of a pencil, but when Laredo told her what they wanted, she smiled and went off to retrieve a small container of vinegar.

'Don't blame me if it doesn't work,' Laredo said. 'It's just what I've heard. I never had one of those myself.'

'A little rubbing in itself is bound to help,' Billy said. He was blushing just a little now. 'Laredo, it's — '

'We've got all day to talk about it,' Laredo said, 'get going! I know she's already here; I saw her come in.'

Laredo sat watching Jesse Goodnight and Bonnie Sue as they lingered at their table. They had no intention of leaving anytime soon. In fact, the man Laredo took for the owner brought out a bottle of chilled wine to them. They still had not budged when Billy returned, shaven, his hair slicked back, his badge gleaming. His blue shirt, the one he had worn along the trail, still showed dirt, but the shiny badge distracted from that. With an air of pride now he swung into his chair, his eyes drifting toward the kitchen.

'She's on the job,' Laredo said. 'She brought me this coffee and I think she was looking for you. You're looking sharp, Billy.'

'Thanks. I see our friends are still here.'

'Just enjoying a lazy afternoon,' Laredo said.

'But why? Why bring Bonnie Sue out in the middle of the day and take her to supper in a popular restaurant?'

'I think Goodnight got tired of looking for Jake Worthy. He decided to try and draw Worthy out into the open by antagonizing the man.'

'Do you think she means that much to Worthy?'

'Who knows? I just know that if Worthy does spot Goodnight — and one of his hired men is bound to — out walking freely in the open with her while Worthy skulks and hides his face, Worthy won't like it one bit. He might take it as a slap in the face. That seems to be what Goodnight is trying to provoke.'

'You mean, Goodnight is ready to just have it out.'

Laredo nodded and took a sip of his coffee. 'Now then, suppose you tell me the story behind the badge.'

* * *

'Seems kind of foolish, doesn't it?' Billy asked. 'Laredo, I was going nowhere, had no job and no prospects. That's

162

why I joined up with the posse, hoping I'd get some sort of reward out of it. Hicks said he liked the way I handled myself taking Hoop Kingman, said he could use a full-time deputy. I know,' — Billy held up a hand — 'you'll say that Hicks only wants a deputy because he's a coward and shouldn't have that job in the first place. He needs someone to do his rough work for him.'

Laredo didn't say anything, nor had he been going to. A man makes his own decisions.

'I maybe like the idea of having a home, Laredo, and a steady job with steady pay.' Again Billy's eyes drifted toward the kitchen. 'I never really have had either.

'I don't have to assume full-time duties until we've finished with the Jake Worthy business. Meantime Hicks said wearing the badge might keep me from getting shot by one of those hired guns. But I mean to stay on in Ellis, Laredo. It's the best thing that could have happened to me.

'You probably take me for a fool, taking a position working for a marshal with no backbone who combs his hair more often than he patrols the streets and shivers at the sound of a gunshot, but, Laredo — '

'I don't think anything about it, Billy. A position is whatever you make it. If you want to take a shot at settling in a town, I think it's fine.'

'It's what I want,' Billy Dewitt said, and he straightened up in his chair, his eyes drifting from Laredo's again. In another minute Nan Singleton arrived at their table with a pot of coffee and an empty cup for Billy. She smiled at him.

'I thought you were just drifting through,' she said in a merry little voice. 'But I see some changes have been made.' She nodded at the badge and Billy grinned. Nan nodded to Laredo and then walked away again, her skirts swishing. It wasn't much of a conversation, but it pleased Billy. His badge had brought him the permanence, the respectability he had wanted to impress Nan with the idea that he was perhaps important enough to speak to.

Billy started to fill both of their cups from the pot. There was the roar of a gun from the street window and Billy dropped the coffee pot. To his left he saw Jesse Goodnight dive to the floor, pulling Bonnie Sue after him. A second shot sounded and a bullet whipped past their table, thudding into the wall behind the cashier, who gave a howl and abandoned his post. As the smoke settled, the owner emerged from the back. They heard him shout, 'Not again!' as he surveyed the shattered window.

Customers were scattering for cover but there were no more shots. An enraged Jesse Goodnight, leaving Bonnie Sue bunched in her skirts on the floor, bolted toward the front door. Billy leaped to his feet to follow. He felt Laredo grab his arm.

'Back door, Billy! You don't run into the guns.'

'Goodnight — '

'Forget Goodnight. He's a fool. Out the back and find our horses because that was Jake Worthy himself doing the shooting. I caught a glimpse of him.'

They darted toward the back door, winding their unfamiliar way past excited cooks and preparation tables. Billy caught a quick glimpse of Nan standing pressed against a far wall, her hands to her lips.

The back door crashed open before Billy's shoulder and Laredo led the way down the alley toward the main street. They were in time to see the tail end of a gray horse turning at the end of the street and heading for open country. Laredo and Billy trotted toward the stable.

'I've seen that horse dozens of times,' Billy panted as they jogged through the heated day. Citizens had collected on the plankwalk, summoned by the gunshots. They must have been wondering what Ellis was coming to with all of the shooting that had been taking place lately.

Laredo finally gasped a reply. 'Worthy's had that horse hitched here and there for days. Hidden in plain sight.'

'Are we going to bother to saddle up?' Billy asked as they stumbled to a halt near the stable doors.

'How far are we going to be riding?' Laredo answered, already grabbing his saddle from the partition.

When his red horse was saddled and ready to go Laredo swung into leather, mentally urging Billy on. The kid's fingers were trembling. He was having trouble with the cinches. Finished at last, Billy swung into the saddle, appearing anxious.

Before they could reach the stable door they saw Jesse Goodnight riding his bay horse past them, stirring up fantails of hot dust.

'Hurry it up. Goodnight must have had his horse at the hitch rail.'

In a few minutes more — though it seemed longer — they were riding out of town in the direction Jake Worthy had taken. They were not alone. Ahead of them they could see Jesse Goodnight flailing at his sleek little bay horse with the ends of his reins. Billy gasped a few words from the back of his blue roan.

'They're gaining distance on us!'

'They can't run those horses at that speed for long,' Laredo said, apparently unconcerned. The ground they crossed over now was beginning to rise. There were fields of scattered red rock underfoot which caused their ponies to stumble. Obviously Worthy had chosen this course for that very reason. Jake Worthy had proven himself to be a thinking man.

Except, perhaps, when it came to Bonnie Sue Garret.

They had no view of Worthy, but as they watched, Goodnight veered sharply off the trail and headed up into the timber flanking the slopes of the rugged hills.

Follow the leader was a fleeting thought in Billy's mind as they swung their horses' heads that way to trail after Goodnight, who was nearer to the fleeing bank robber. And he considered with some irony that if it were not for Goodnight's fast start they might have already lost Worthy's trail.

That makes two of them we'll have to fight was what Billy Dewitt was thinking. What was on Laredo's mind was unknown. He rode on with determination on his face and a sure hand on the reins of his red roan, his eyes fixed on the fleeing men ahead of them. Or on the dust they were leaving behind, because as the two badmen entered the tall pines, they became hidden from view, screened by the trees.

Billy Dewitt's blue roan was laboring beneath him before they topped out the hill. He sat his horse among a cluster of gray granite boulders under a massive cedar tree that had grown up among the rocks. His horse's flanks heaved between his legs as the animal gasped for air. They had lost the trail; that was obvious, but it seemed not to bother Laredo, who had stepped down briefly from his red horse to give the horse a little extra relief.

'Whenever you're ready,' Laredo said.

'Which way? Laredo, you know we've lost them.'

'You're right,' Laredo answered, unperturbed. 'As we intended to. We'll be riding down now,' he said, pointing toward the grassy valley below. 'There's no sense continuing to ride the skyline. It's rugged and slow-going. The only reason Jake Worthy led us up here is to throw us off his trail. He won't stay among the rocks and timber for long — he's got places to go. We'll go down and meet him when he gets there.'

It seemed to Billy that this was only a guess, but Laredo showed no doubts, and Billy had to admit the logic of it. Worthy was not going to be reaching his goal — whatever that was — by this slow riding through timber, skirting the massive stacks of stone which dominated the slopes.

Billy only nodded his agreement. The

blue roan's labored breathing had settled to a more normal rate. They started their horses down the pine-clad slope, weaving their way through the concealing timber, their horses now and then slipping on the fallen pine needles. Shadows flickered across them, the big trees casting deep, cool darkness and alternately allowing brilliant shafts of golden sunlight to touch them.

The timber thinned and then fell away as they reached the bottom of the slope. There was a narrow silver rill winding its way across the grassy valley and Laredo walked his horse to water.

'We have the time,' he told Billy. 'It'll be awhile before Worthy can be sure he's shaken off Goodnight and make his way down the slope.'

Billy thought that Laredo sounded too damn sure of himself at times like these, and he wouldn't have minded seeing the tall man proven wrong. Knowing that this was an unworthy thought, Billy only nodded and looked toward the hills behind and beside them, wondering which way Worthy would use to get down.

'Let's cross the valley,' Laredo said. 'We'll wait at the forest verge. He won't see us there, and hopefully he'll believe he's lost us in the high country.'

They dismounted at the edge of the forest, the shade of the pine trees cool as the day went on. A wind rustled the treetops. The bluejays and red squirrels that had been disturbed upon the arrival of the horsemen now returned to their private affairs, twittering and chattering, fluttering and leaping in the trees.

The minutes passed slowly. Billy was chilled, hungry, frustrated. Laredo continued to crouch beside his horse, holding its reins, his eyes fixed constantly on the hills surrounding the valley. The man had incredible patience but then he would have cultivated it over the years.

As Billy watched, a squirrel wound its way down a pine tree. Reaching the ground it sat up and sniffed the air. Its eyes met Billy Dewitt's and seemed to register shock. It darted up the tree in sheer panic and despite the tension surrounding them, Billy laughed.

'Having fun?' Laredo asked in a low voice. He rose to his feet, stretching his leg muscles.

'Not much,' Billy said, leaning across his saddle. 'This is it, isn't it? I mean this is what you do for a living.'

'Pretty much,' Laredo answered.

Billy said, 'There's a man out there somewhere in a hundred square miles of timber, and you want him. It might be hopeless, but if it is, you'll go on.' Laredo nodded. 'Most of your work is running out wild goose chases, and if you get lucky and find your man, it leads to real trouble, gun trouble.'

'Most of the time. I have had a few men just give me the money to return. There was a cashier who had just gone a little berserk and left town one day with a suitcase full of cash. He'd had a change of heart and was happy to just have me return it to the bank for him.'

Billy thought about that for a moment and then asked, 'How many cases have you had like that, Laredo?'

The tall man grinned, thumbed back his hat and said, 'Not many.'

'That's just it,' Billy said. 'Most of these men would sooner shoot you on sight. That's what I mean — chasing all over the countryside looking for a man you hope won't kill you when you find him. I'd rather be a town lawman where I know every street and every person. Have a home to go back to every night, you know, Laredo?' Billy said.

'I understand, and it seems you've made the best choice. Things might work out well in Ellis.'

'They have to,' Billy said with determination.

'You're still with me on this one, finding Jake Worthy.'

'That's what I started out to do,' Dewitt said, 'and I'll do it.'

'Step into leather, then. Here's our chance.'

As Billy let his eyes go in the

direction Laredo was looking, he saw the lone rider. A featureless man in the distance, walking a weary gray horse along the rill that flowed across the grassy valley. It was Jake Worthy. Finally.

Billy Dewitt tightened his saddle cinches and loosened the Colt in his holster. Now he was finally going to get to observe Laredo at work. Jake Worthy was no meek bank cashier, and he wasn't going to willingly hand over the small fortune he was carrying in his saddle-bags. There would be smoke in the meadow and probably blood staining the bright green grass that grew there.

10

The gray horse was clear in vision. It had a somewhat heavy, long-loping stride they were familiar with since Ellis. The man riding had a slumped posture and as Billy studied his shadowed face, he seemed older than he had believed Jake Worthy to be, and seemed wearier. He had shaven off his mustache and wore his holster on his left side.

'It's your call,' Billy said to Laredo.

Laredo gave him a look of surprise. 'There's no call to make. We're sure not going to bushwhack the man, so let's ride out and meet him. You might want to unpin that shiny badge of yours, though.'

Billy took a deep breath, unpinned his badge and stuffed it into his shirt pocket. Then, reluctantly, he kneed his blue roan forward, following Laredo out onto the grassland. Jake Worthy's head jerked upright and they saw him shift in his saddle. His face was grim as he rode on, but he did not alter his course or try to run for it. Perhaps he didn't feel his horse was up to it. Maybe Worthy himself wasn't.

Laredo drew up his horse and waited, Billy beside and slightly behind him. A stiff wind was flattening the grass, ruffling the silver face of the winding rill. Two crows wheeled past, cawing raucously, their shadows swift and ominous against the grass.

Laredo waited, his hands crossed on his saddle pommel. He seemed to have no concerns. The time for worrying and planning had passed. Billy Dewitt tried to emulate Laredo's calmness, but his nerves were jittery, his stomach balled into a knot. Laredo waited until Worthy was a mere fifty feet from them, then he called out.

'Hello, Jake! Pull up a minute, will you? We need to talk.'

'I don't know you,' Jake Worthy grumbled.

'No matter. I've been sent out here to talk to you. It's in your best interests to listen to what I have to say.'

Jake Worthy was only two horse-lengths away now, the gray drawn up. He eyed Laredo carefully and then asked, 'Are you out of Tucson?'

'That's right,' Laredo answered.

'That's something I could never have figured on,' he muttered. Worthy's eyes flickered briefly to Billy Dewitt, then returned to Laredo. 'All right, have your say. That's what they pay you for.'

'If you know who I am, you know what I'm going to say,' Laredo replied slowly. 'Hand over the money and you can be on your way.'

'Do you think I'm crazy?' Worthy exploded.

'I wouldn't know,' Laredo answered. 'Are you?'

'After all I've been through, you can't believe I'd just hand this over.'

'It would leave you no worse off than you were when you started,' Laredo pointed out. 'You know I won't arrest you, Worthy, not even for killing the man in the bank.'

'That Abel Skinner. He was an idiot. He tried to take my gun away from me.'

'None of that matters to me,' Laredo said. 'Just hand over what's left of the loot and you can go on your way.'

'Do many do that?' Worthy asked.

'Not many,' Laredo told him. 'Only the smart ones.'

'Look, even if I was of a mind to be a good boy and do as you ask, I recognize the kid here, and back in Ellis I saw him wearing a badge. There was plenty of lead spent back there. Ellis law would sure arrest me.'

Laredo spoke for Billy, 'You're not in Ellis now, Worthy. His badge doesn't mean a thing. It's only me you have to satisfy and the money will do that.'

'You know, what you say makes sense,' Worthy said, scratching at his long chin. 'The thing is . . . '

That was as far as Jake Worthy got. As they watched he dropped his hand toward his big Colt revolver, drew and fired. The bullet whipped by Laredo's head, coming within inches of doing its job. It was, however, only wasted lead, as Laredo drew and fired in one fluid movement that left Billy suitably impressed. The .44 slug from Laredo's pistol slammed into Jake Worthy's chest, lifted him in the saddle and left him to slump and fall to the ground as his startled horse danced away.

Billy slipped from his saddle, gun in hand, and approached Worthy's body. He crouched over the man, felt for a pulse and found none. He turned to Laredo, the wind bending back the brim of his hat.

'Is that the way it usually works?' Billy asked.

'Except when the man's a better shot than I am,' Laredo said. 'Catch up to that horse, Billy, and yank the saddle-bags from it. If you want Jake Worthy's body to take back to Ellis, I'll help you throw him over.'

'What use have I got for him but as a trophy?'

'In your situation it might be to your advantage to have a trophy to show. Let folks know you're fit for the job.'

'I'm not the one who shot him,' Billy exclaimed, leading the gray horse back to where Laredo waited.

'Weren't you? In all of the excitement, I can't remember who got him,' Laredo said, thumbing a fresh cartridge into his pistol. 'Anyway, I have no use for him, and it's that or leave him to the birds.' Laredo nodded toward the crows who were now circling closer. There were now seven of them, and farther away, wingtips spread against the wind, the dark form of an approaching buzzard could be seen against the pale sky.

'Here you go,' Billy said, handing up the saddle-bags that Worthy had been carrying. Laredo tossed them over his horse's neck. 'Aren't you going to check it out, count up the money?'

'What for? I can't recover any more than he had, and whatever's left of that is in here. They've got a whole office full of people in Tucson who spend their time counting dollars. It's their job, not mine.'

'It's a long ride back carrying all that money,' Billy said.

'I won't be carrying it. I'll have it freighted to Quirt from Ellis. My report, when I get around to writing it, will simply read, 'Found Quirt robber. Funds recovered.' That's all.'

'No details at all?' Billy asked.

'They don't pay me for writing stories, Billy. I'm not even riding to Tucson after I've taken care of those two matters. I'm headed straight back to my woman in Crater. Tucson can make of it what they will.'

The familiar voice called to them from the pine-woods. 'Thanks for the assistance, men,' Jesse Goodnight said, emerging from the trees on his lathered bay horse, his rifle in his hands. 'I would have rather shot the man down myself, but I'm grateful for small favors. Shuck those pistols, boys, and let the saddle-bags drop, Riley!'

Since the man behind them held a cocked Winchester on them, there wasn't a lot of point in arguing the point and no sense trying to delay the inevitable.

Laredo spoke as Goodnight walked his faltering pony forward. 'I didn't think you could keep up with the man.'

'Neither did he. Why don't you both slip to the ground, and Riley, you can hand those saddle-bags up to me.'

'All right,' Laredo said agreeably, swinging his leg over the horse's neck and sliding to the ground, hands held high.

Laredo unslung the saddle-bags from his horse's neck and handed them up to Goodnight. His bay horse shied slightly. It, too, was obviously fatigued. Goodnight had lost his hat along the trail and the breeze shifted his dark hair. There was a smile on his thin lips, but it was not a nice expression.

'I'd like to thank you men for — '

The sharp crack of a Winchester rifle wiped out the rest of the sentence. Its following echo rolled across the valley.

Jesse Goodnight lay sprawled on his back against the grass, only a few feet from where Jake Worthy had fallen. Neither man moved nor would move again. Billy's eyes had gone wide, and he grabbed for his pistol.

As the man with the rifle emerged from the forest, Laredo clasped his hand around Billy's wrist. 'You won't be needing that, Billy,' he said in a soft voice.

'But . . . ' Billy had to take Laredo's word for it. His hand fell away from his pistol as the man approached them. Billy squinted into the sun, which was beaming through the pines. He had seen this man before, but where . . . ?

The stranger was lanky. He wore a shabby green jacket and had a growth of salt-and-pepper whiskers across his hollow jowls. His blue eyes were piercing. His lips were curled in a smile of satisfaction.

'Finally got him, did you?' Laredo said.

'I was afraid you were going to take him first,' the man with the rifle said. 'I didn't want it that way.'

'I know,' Laredo answered.

'You know who I am?' the rifleman said with surprise.

'I guessed it,' Laredo nodded.

Billy was nervous, upset. 'Well, I'm a bad guesser. Why doesn't one of you tell me who this fellow is?'

'Sorry,' the man with the rifle said, lowering his weapon as he toed Goodnight's body. 'The name is Klotz. Zachary Klotz. Goodnight killed my brother, Adonis, in Quirt five years ago over a gambling debt. Shot him down in an alley. This one,' he said, nodding at Worthy's body, 'was there watching.

'Adonis was a gambler, but never a cheat. Jesse Goodnight should have been hanged, but he wasn't. Five years in prison was all they gave him. I waited those five years out. When I heard he was back in Quirt I knew it was time for me to make it up for my brother.'

'You followed the posse,' Billy said, understanding, 'riding the high ground.'

'Yes. I apologize for shooting up your

campfire that night. I was just frustrated, couldn't get a clear shot at Goodnight. Now,' he paused, 'I got it.' He asked Laredo, 'Do you want me for anything?'

'No.'

'What about you?' he asked Billy, and Billy shook his head silently. Klotz turned on his heel and slowly walked back to the forest, re-entering it silently.

'The man nursed a long anger,' Billy said, picking up the saddle-bags again, handing them to Laredo.

'He did,' Laredo agreed. 'Good thing for us, as it turned out. All right, shall we throw these two over their ponies' backs and get started toward Ellis?'

'I suppose we'd better,' Billy said. 'Think we can make it by supper time?'

'It doesn't matter,' Laredo said. 'Nan will be around somewhere, waiting for you.'

'Makes you think about Bonnie Sue Garret, doesn't it?' Billy commented as they got to their task, hoisting Jake Worthy's body onto his gray's back.

'What do you mean?'

'Well, she was playing both ends against the middle, figuring that whichever one won out she'd be richer for it.'

'She was,' Laredo said, knotting one of the ropes under the belly of Worthy's gray horse to hold his ankles and wrists in place. 'Bonnie Sue should have learned what most card players know. Doubling down on your bets doesn't guarantee success.'

They reached Ellis just as the last glow of a spectacular sunset faded from the western skies. Billy had reattached his badge to his shirt, and their appearance with two men tied across their saddles drew onlookers all up and down the street. The sight of the law in Ellis returning with men captured or dead was a rare occurrence, since everyone knew Marshal Hicks preferred to do his law-enforcing from the comfort of his swivel chair.

'We're in time for supper after all,' Laredo said, pleased at the prospect of a hot meal.

Billy looked uncertain. 'I hope so, I don't know what kind of paperwork and such this requires.' He nodded his head toward the tethered horses they were leading.

'Let Hicks worry about all of that. Nan will be waiting and watching.'

'You think so?' Billy's face brightened and then went glum again.

'Yes, I do, now get over these negative feelings. You've got a job, almost have a girl, you've got your work finished.'

'I know, Laredo, but it's happened all at once. Remember, Hicks told me that I was to start my regular duties as soon as this Worthy business was cleared up.'

'He won't mean tonight, Billy. I can tell him I need you to help me clean up one last matter.'

'What matter?'

'There is none. Unless you can count eating supper with me. Tomorrow is soon enough for you to start worrying about your new job.'

In his office Hicks looked both pleased and excited to see them. He frowned as he looked outside at the bodies of the two badmen, but brightened as he thought of it burnishing his reputation.

Laredo didn't need to use his lie on Hicks. The marshal was as pleased as if he had done the rough work himself. He was strutting around in his office, rubbing his palms together. 'Good job,' he said to Billy. 'Don't worry about the rest of it. I'll see that those two get planted.'

He practically shoved them out the door. Laredo thought the marshal wanted to be alone to take credit for the Worthy capture when the local citizens began arriving to ask questions. It didn't matter to Laredo, and it suited Billy, who only took the time to ask Hicks, 'I see you've lost your prisoner. Where's Hoop Kingman?'

'I talked to the judge and was informed that there's no case against Kingman, and we shouldn't have even brought him in. I expect Hoop's back over at the saloon by now. Don't worry about it, Billy. Everyone knows you did your best.'

Billy exchanged a look with Laredo and then without another word they went out to the hitch rail, untied their horses and led them up the street toward the hotel restaurant.

'I guess that's the way things are going to go with Hicks,' Billy said. 'He'll take all the credit; I'll get all the blame.'

'It seems like it. Can you take it, Billy?'

'So long as they pay me steady, Laredo, I can take anything.'

After they had eaten, with Billy hovered over by an anxious Nan Singleton, Laredo pushed back from the table and rose. 'I've got things to see to,' he said, but neither seemed to hear him. He left Billy to tell the doting girl all about his adventures, and went out into the cool of night. He carried the saddle-bags filled with stolen money to the freight office, gave it into their care and got a receipt from a narrow, balding man who tried to sound confidence-inspiring. Laredo listened awhile to a talk on their safety record and then nodded and went out to look for the telegraph office. The message he sent to Tucson was worded almost exactly as he had told Billy earlier: 'Found Quirt bank robber. Funds recovered. Laredo.'

Considering he had finished the job before they had even contacted him about it, Laredo figured he was due for a good long vacation. As he walked along the cool street toward the hotel, he found himself thinking of his wife, Dusty. What a treasure that patient, red-headed woman was.

There was no light in Billy's hotel room when he passed it in the hallway. Laredo managed to get his boots off and unbuckle his gunbelt before his head hit the pillow and he fell into a restful sleep with the cool breeze wafting through the slightly open window of his room.

The end of a job was always the best part of it, sleep the best reward.

11

'You'll never guess!' Billy Dewitt said breathlessly after knocking on and swinging open Laredo's door in the early hours of the morning. The sun had just crept over the horizon, spraying golden fans through the cottonwood trees outside his window. Laredo yawned, scratched his head and sat up in bed.

'What?' he asked the obviously excited kid.

'Last night I took Nan home,' he said, taking a seat on Laredo's bed as Laredo rose to wash his face and comb his hair. Laredo watched Billy's flushed face in the mirror. He had nothing to say. Billy went on, 'I met her mother, Roxie. We all had a little talk.'

'About?' Laredo asked, drying his face. He reached for his gunbelt and slung it around his waist.

'Well,' Billy answered hesitantly, 'it's

like this — they both think that I should set my mind on being the town marshal.' In a rush of words, he continued, 'They were saying that no one much likes the way Marshal Hicks goes about his job, or rather, doesn't go about it. They told me that everyone in town knows he's lazy, and that I was new blood, showing a lot of spunk.'

'It's nice to have people admire you,' Laredo said, for something to say.

'Yes.' Billy's excitement was not waning. 'Well, Roxie said that everyone knows I had worked under Sheriff Will Fawcett and that it was me who braced Hoop Kingman in the saloon and not Hicks.' Billy stopped for breath. He smiled shyly at Laredo as he was putting on his hat. 'And Roxie says that it was me who brought in the Quirt bank robber and that no-good Jesse Goodnight. Everyone knows that, they were telling me, and they would be sure to speak up for me the next time the marshal's position is open.

'First, though, Roxie says I should

spend some time as deputy under Hicks to get to know the people in town and how Hicks handles his paperwork and such so that I'll be ready when the time comes.'

'That's sensible,' Laredo said. It seemed that Roxie Singleton was a woman who watched out for her daughter's prospects. All right, she sounded pushy, but maybe that was what Billy needed just now. It was no wonder the youngster was flying high. He had a job, a future and a woman to dream on. A week ago he had been sitting broke and without direction in a Quirt saloon.

Laredo made no comments, and it was doubtful that Billy expected any. Laredo was only a sounding board, someone he could share his happiness with.

'Have you got time to get some breakfast, Billy?'

'I don't report to Hicks until eight o'clock, so yes, Laredo. Let's eat.'

The morning sun was still low in their eyes when they walked out of the restaurant. It was a good enough meal of ham and eggs, biscuits and gravy, but Laredo hadn't lingered over it as an eager Nan Singleton hovered over Billy as if he were the only person in the place. Laredo had never been fond of being the third party around a romantic couple. Billy was sent off as if he were a boy on his first day at school, with Nan waving goodbye from the restaurant door.

'What are you going to do this morning, Laredo?'

'See to my horse, make sure the package got off, see if I got a reply to my telegram. I might even drop by the doctor's and see how Lester Burnett is doing. I figure I can pay his bill and get myself reimbursed later. Maybe we don't even owe Burnett that, but he was with the posse, and he is a broke and wounded man.

'Then I'll pick up a few supplies and get started on my way south.'

'Had enough of Ellis already?'

'It's not that so much. It's just that I do have a place I'd rather be. It's called home.'

'I understand,' Billy said. He paused

as they stepped into the street across from the stable. 'I'd like to thank you, Laredo. You taught me some things without me even knowing you were teaching.'

'Whatever you mean, you're welcome,' Laredo said warmly. 'You were a good trail partner.'

They were shaking hands when the long shadow cast by the low sun crossed over them. Laredo tensed instantly and stepped aside. Billy turned toward the bulky form of a drunken Hoop Kingman. He had a leer on his flushed face and a cold glint in his glazed eyes. His hands were wrapped menacingly around a twelve-gauge shotgun.

'You didn't really think you were done with me, did you, *deputy?*'

'Why not?' Billy tried, though he was visibly shaken. 'What's the point in carrying this on?'

'The point is,' Hoop Kingman said, stepping forward, his hands tightening on the shotgun, 'you made a fool out of me in front of my friends . . . and there's the other.'

'The other? What other?' Billy asked blankly.

'There's money on both your heads, you knew that.'

'Jake Worthy is dead, Kingman, he can't pay you now.'

'Jake Worthy is dead but the money isn't gone,' Kingman said. His eyes narrowed. 'Worthy had a certain fund tucked away. He couldn't be seen handing out gold on the street, could he? He left money in good hands in case he decided that it was time for him to make a run for it. The money was to be paid to anyone who took out the remaining posse members — and that means the two of you.

'So you see, deputy, there is still a point in this. You two are worth a hundred dollars in gold money to me. I know the man who's holding the money; you don't need his name, and it won't matter in about five seconds.'

Farther along the street Billy could see, or imagined he could see, Nan Singleton leaning out of a doorway to watch them. Billy said shakily, 'You can't shoot down a lawman in broad daylight and expect to get away with it.'

'Sure I can. I've got my horse saddled and the money's ready for me. What do I have to fear? Marshal Hicks coming after me?' Hoop Kingman's lips formed a rubbery, disparaging smile. King-man's thumb drew back both hammers of the double-twelve and he shouldered the scattergun. Billy Dewitt glanced wildly at Laredo, who had not moved a finger, and then, almost in a panic, Billy went for his holstered Colt.

There would be time for only one shot before the shotgun's loads cut them in half, Billy knew, and he determined to make that shot count. If his draw was not quick, it was barely good enough to do the job. As Hoop Kingman's thick finger tightened on the shotgun triggers, Billy Dewitt's hastily fired shot ripped through Hoop's throat. His head jerked back; the muzzle of the shotgun lifted high and was touched off, erupting with flame, smoke and buckshot. A nearby awning lost a chunk of wood. A horse panicked and reared up at the hitch rail. From down the street a long, piercing cry rose from a woman's throat and Nan Singleton came running as Hoop Kingman's body leaked blood and lay unmoving in the street.

'Well?' Billy Dewitt finally demanded as they sat sipping coffee at the restaurant. There was still quite a stir around them, though most of the uproar the death of Hoop Kingman had caused had died down.

Laredo looked up at Billy with hooded eyes. 'Well what?'

'You know what I mean, Laredo,' the blond kid said. 'You didn't draw on Hoop; you weren't even ready to shoot. I saw you.'

Laredo shrugged slightly. 'What's the sense in both of us shooting him?' he asked.

'How could you know that I was going to be quick enough, that I even had the heart to make my try against a shotgun?'

'I figured you did. It's your town, Billy. You're the one they pay to keep law and order. I take care of business when I have to. This was your time.'

'You might have been killed!' Billy said powerfully.

'I didn't think so. I trusted you. Now you've got to trust yourself, make the whole town trust you.'

'You're not telling me you let me do it for the glory!' Billy said, half-laughing.

'No, I'm saying that there's a time when a man shouldn't need a teacher any longer, when he knows that it's his time to shine.'

Laredo got to his feet and fished for a silver dollar in the pocket of his jeans. He nodded, flipped the coin onto the table and said, 'It's your time, Billy.'

Then Laredo turned and was gone, his shadow casting a brief memory against the wooden floor of the restaurant.

THE END

We do hope that you have enjoyed reading this large print book.

Did you know that all of our titles are available for purchase?

We publish a wide range of high quality large print books including:
Romances, Mysteries, Classics
General Fiction
Non Fiction and Westerns

Special interest titles available in large print are:
The Little Oxford Dictionary
Music Book, Song Book
Hymn Book, Service Book

Also available from us courtesy of Oxford University Press:
Young Readers' Dictionary
(large print edition)
Young Readers' Thesaurus
(large print edition)

For further information or a free brochure, please contact us at:
Ulverscroft Large Print Books Ltd.,
The Green, Bradgate Road, Anstey,
Leicester, LE7 7FU, England.
Tel: (00 44) **0116 236 4325**
Fax: (00 44) **0116 234 0205**

Seth Klugg, manager of the Spring-field Cattlemen's Bank, is out of town, seeing the proposed new railroad as an opportunity for drumming up business. Meanwhile, the three strangers who ride into Springfield see in his absence an opportunity of their own . . . Kidnapping the assistant bank manager and his wife, they proceed to hold them hostage, awaiting the return of Klugg — the only man who knows the combination for the bank's safe. But Klugg has made many enemies, and is riding alone across open terrain — what will happen if he fails to return?